"There's No Reason Why We Can't Share The Bed, Zeke."

"Don't kid yourself, Angie. There's an excellent reason. I don't have the energy or the willpower to leave you tonight if things get overheated...and I can't imagine sharing a bed with you and *not* having things get overheated."

Zeke walked to the door and paused, looking back. "I'm going to see if this place has a shower. Don't open the door for anyone, understand?"

Angie nodded as he left. She sat there hugging herself. Never had it occurred to her that they wouldn't find comfortable rooms to spend the night.

Her traitorous body had already acknowledged awareness of their situation. She was aware of every move Zeke made, every breath he took, every word he said. She felt as though, even if she were blindfolded, she would be able to find him in a crowd...just by the very essence of who he was.

Dear Reader,

Check out the hot hunks on the covers of this month's Desire books. These are our RED, WHITE AND BLUE heroes, and they sure are something, aren't they? These guys are red-blooded, white-knight, blue-collar types, and they're guaranteed to make the hot summer nights even *hotter!*

Next month, we have a new title from Diana Palmer that I know you'll all enjoy. It's called *Night of Love,* and as an extra bonus it's *also* August's *Man of the Month* title. Also coming up in August are titles from Dixie Browning, Lass Small, Linda Turner, Barbara McCauley and Cathie Linz. Don't miss a single one.

And I'm still waiting for answers to last month's questions. What exactly do you like in Desire? Is there anything we can do differently? Do more of? *Less* of? No answer is too outrageous!

So, until next month, enjoy! And don't forget to let me know how you feel.

Lucia Macro
Senior Editor

ANNETTE BROADRICK
ZEKE

SILHOUETTE *Desire*®

Published by Silhouette Books New York

America's Publisher of Contemporary Romance

SILHOUETTE BOOKS
300 East 42nd St., New York, N.Y. 10017

ZEKE

Copyright © 1993 by Annette Broadrick

ISBN: 0-373-05793-8

First Silhouette Books printing July 1993

All the characters in this book have no existence outside the
imagination of the author and have no relation whatsoever to
anyone bearing the same name or names. They are not even
distantly inspired by any individual known or unknown to the
author, and all incidents are pure invention.

® and ™:Trademarks used with authorization. Trademarks
indicated with ® are registered in the United States Patent and
Trademark Office, the Canada Trade Mark Office and in other
countries.

Printed in the U.S.A.

Books by Annette Broadrick

Silhouette Desire

Hunter's Prey #185
Bachelor Father #219
Hawk's Flight #242
Deceptions #272
Choices #283
Heat of the Night #314
Made in Heaven #336
Return to Yesterday #360
Adam's Story #367
Momentary Marriage #414
With All My Heart #433
A Touch of Spring #464
Irresistible #499
A Loving Spirit #552
Candlelight for Two #577
Lone Wolf #666
Where There Is Love #714
*Love Texas Style! #734
*Courtship Texas Style! #739
*Marriage Texas Style! #745
Zeke #793

*Sons of Texas

Silhouette Romance

Circumstantial Evidence #329
Provocative Peril #359
Sound of Summer #412
Unheavenly Angel #442
Strange Enchantment #501
Mystery Lover #533
That's What Friends Are For #544
Come Be My Love #609
A Love Remembered #676
Married?! #742
The Gemini Man #796

Silhouette Books

Silhouette Christmas Stories 1988
"Christmas Magic"

Spring Fancy 1993
"Surprise, Surprise!"

ANNETTE BROADRICK

lives on the shores of Lake of the Ozarks in Missouri, where she spends her time doing what she loves most—reading and writing romance fiction. Since 1984, when her first book was published, Annette has been delighting her readers with her imaginative and innovative style. In addition to being nominated by *Romantic Times* magazine as one of the Best New Authors of that year, she has also won the *Romantic Times* Reviewer's Choice Award for Best in its Series for *Heat of the Night, Mystery Lover* and *Irresistible,* the *Romantic Times* WISH Award for her hero in *Strange Enchantment* and the *Romantic Times* Lifetime Achievement Award for Series Romance.

I dedicated my first book, written in 1983, to Lynn Jordan and Lauraine Snelling, acknowledging the fact that without their assistance and encouragement I would never have been able to finish and polish that first effort of mine.

Now, nine years and thirty-four books later, Lynn and Lauraine have once again come through with encouragement, advice and steadfast support to keep me going when the going gets rough.

Thank you both for always being there for me. I couldn't have done it without you.

Annette Broadrick

Prologue

Zeke strode down one of the many hallways that formed the maze of offices of his headquarters. Since he'd had little reason to visit the place during the years he'd worked for the agency, he clutched a hand-drawn map in his fist.

He was a field man because that's what he wanted. He enjoyed being on his own, making his own decisions, following up on leads in his own way.

His reports were timely filed with the appropriate individuals and quickly dismissed from his mind. He abhorred paperwork of any kind. He assumed that after he passed on information, it was carefully analyzed and eventually fell onto the proper desk in the prescribed manner.

The fact that he was in the Virginia office at all was proof that the world had changed in a radical way. He was still having difficulty adjusting to some of those changes. Why, the KGB were giving visitors tours through their facilities, for crying out loud! For all he knew, the Langley headquarters had just been purchased by Disney for use as another one of its amusement parks.

So where did that leave him? What was there left for a man of his background and training in covert operations to do?

He rounded a corner, frowned at the map in his hand, checked the numbers and arrows posted along the wall, then proceeded down the next hallway.

Maybe they planned to offer him a position as a tour guide.

When he found the number he was looking for, he tapped on the door before opening it. A woman sat at a desk, working at a computer. She looked up when he came through the doorway, and smiled. "Mr. Daniels?"

"Yep."

"Please go on in. Mr. Carpenter is expecting you."

Zeke nodded, opened the next door and found himself in a comfortable-looking office. Although he had never been there before, he recognized the man behind the desk speaking on the phone. Frank Carpenter had been his superior for more than ten years. Whenever they met person to person, Frank, usually dressed as a tourist, had always come to him in whatever part of the world he happened to be. This was the first time he'd seen his boss in a suit and tie, looking for all the world like a typical businessman.

Frank waved him to one of the chairs and Zeke sat down. He always felt out of place in this type of environment, which was the biggest reason he had turned down the promotions he'd been offered in the past. He had known that a promotion would mean being assigned a desk and an office of his own. He had a sinking feeling that he was about to be offered such a position once again.

He'd rather be a tour guide at a Disney facility.

Frank hung up the phone, stood and walked around the desk with his hand extended. "Good to see you, Zeke. You're looking a hell of a lot better these days than the last time I saw you."

Zeke stood and took the offered hand. "That's not too surprising, considering I'd just had a couple of metal fragments removed from vital parts of my anatomy."

"I was worried about you," Frank admitted. "I felt I needed to be there to be certain you were going to recover fully. Had any residual problems?"

"Except for a knee that gives accurate weather reports, I'm okay."

"Glad to hear it." Frank studied him for a moment before returning to his chair behind the desk. "You didn't have any trouble finding my office, did you?"

Zeke smiled blandly. "I had them draw me a map at the front entrance...and I left a trail of bread crumbs so I would have no difficulty finding my way out of here."

Frank leaned back in his chair, still studying Zeke. "You're really looking fit, I'm glad to see. A little leaner, maybe, but that's probably healthier. The report of your last medical checkup could have been of a man nearly twenty years younger."

Zeke lifted an eyebrow. "You've so little to do these days that you're poring over medical reports to relieve the monotony?"

"Actually, we've been quite busy around here. There's always a need for intelligence reports from around the world . . . always something brewing."

"So why the scrutiny into my physical condition? Are you thinking about calling me in on a permanent basis?" Zeke looked around the room, futilely trying to imagine himself working in a similar environment.

"On the contrary, I've received a rather urgent request to lend you to another branch of the government."

Zeke's usually quick tongue betrayed him, causing him to stare at his superior in surprised silence.

"I don't know how well you've been able to keep abreast of the news in this hemisphere during the past few years," Frank began, "but we've got another kind of war on our hands here in the States . . . a drug war."

Zeke leaned back in his chair, straightened his long legs and crossed his ankles. "I would've had to have been on the moon not to have heard that piece of news. Come to think of it, even there I could probably have picked up some of the satellite transmissions."

"The Drug Enforcement Administration has doubled, almost tripled, its agents along the Texas-Mexico border in an effort to stop the incoming flood of drugs. In beefing up their operations, however, they've managed to develop more problems."

"Such as?"

"They are very much afraid that some of the agents have discovered a sizable second income by looking the other way when a big shipment is due from one of the Mexican cartels . . . at least that's what some of the department heads in this area are beginning to suspect."

"But they can't prove it."

"No. There are still numerous arrests being made from Brownsville to El Paso and points in between. In charting those arrests, the DEA discovered that most of them were small-time drug runners, some college kids looking for thrills and extra cash, and an occasional expendable member of one of the Colombian cartels. What has them on edge is that despite all their efforts, they've never been able to get anything on Lorenzo De la Garza."

"De la Garza? Who is he?"

"He's a wealthy businessman who lives near Monterrey and owns several factories scattered throughout Mexico. After he gathers the raw product—everything from wool to mineral ore to wood—he turns it into salable merchandise and exports the products made."

"Sounds legitimate to me."

"It's supposed to. About two years ago the agency received an anonymous tip that De la Garza was using his established shipping routes to smuggle drugs. Since they check out every piece of information received, the DEA set up a surveillance on random shipments coming through customs. Although traces of drugs were found on two separate occasions, there wasn't enough evidence to make any arrests.

"The DEA decided to place some agents around De la Garza in an effort to find out more about his operation. Although those agents have been reporting for almost a year now, they insist they can find no evidence to link his organization with drugs. However, his shipments have increased substantially and he continues to expand his business."

"So where do I come in?"

"The DEA is afraid that De la Garza has bought off their agents. In return, he's being alerted to which shipments will be checked for drugs. The agency came to me with the idea of placing someone inside De la Garza's organization who no one in their group knows to find out who's passing on information. I thought of you."

"You want me to go undercover on a drug operation?"

"Yes."

"Pretending to be what, exactly?"

Frank smiled. "Yourself, with some slight modifications in your work history. We suggest that you present yourself as a mercenary, bored with inaction, and offer your services. De la Garza's been having security problems lately, that much we've learned. He could use a man with your skills to help him. Once you get inside his operation, you'll be able to gain access to his files, find out who's on the take . . . that sort of thing. In essence you'll be spying on the spies." Frank closed the file in front of him. "The DEA wants verification of what they suspect is happening. They want to nail whoever is giving De la Garza information on their movements along the border. Of course, if you happen to get your hands on enough evidence to get De la Garza at the same time, they won't complain."

Zeke shook his head. "They don't ask much, do they?"

Frank shrugged. "They wanted our best agent, which is why I recommended you. You've gained quite a reputation in the business over the years, you know. Of course, De la Garza will do a check on your background. He's a smart man or he wouldn't be where he is today. What we intend to do is publicize your exploits to the right people, play up your nickname, that sort of thing. I don't think you'll have a problem getting hired."

Zeke eyed his boss with a hint of wariness. "What, exactly, is my nickname?"

Frank smiled. "I thought you knew. The opposition began to call you 'The Intimidator,' a few years ago. Guess the tag stuck."

"The Intimidator? Where did that come from?"

Frank shook his head. "Who knows where it started? The interesting point about it is that everyone immediately knew who they were referring to—you."

"You've got to be joking."

"Nope."

Zeke tugged on his earlobe. "I don't go around intimidating people."

"You think not? Some people think you can read minds, know when they're lying or hiding something. They find that particular kind of talent downright intimidating, but we don't need to tell De la Garza how you got that nickname."

"So let me get this straight. I'm to walk up to this guy and offer my services. If and when he hires me, I'm supposed to figure out which agents he's got on his payroll and, incidentally, gather enough hard evidence to nail him in U.S. courts. You think he's going to let some stranger learn all his secrets?"

"I don't think he'll have a choice once you're in there."

Zeke slowly sat up in his chair and leaned his elbows on his knees. "I don't suppose you have any ideas about how I can accomplish this assignment, do you?"

Frank grinned. "A few. I've already requested files on every one of their field agents so that you can familiarize yourself with their descriptions." He nodded to a stack of folders piled on the side of his desk. "In addition, I've thought of a way to use your background to benefit the role I have in mind for you."

"I'm listening."

"We could let it be known that we're terminating you with harsh feelings on both sides. As a soldier of fortune with an extensive background in intelligence work, you might find your talents in high demand in certain circles."

"That's always good to know," Zeke drawled. "Job security is always reassuring, I suppose."

Frank thumbed open another file and glanced at its contents. "Another reason you're a good choice is because you were born in South Texas. You grew up speaking both languages fluently. You know the area. I understand you used to do some camping and fishing in the mountains down in Mexico as a teenager."

Zeke's jaw tightened. "Yeah. I had a good friend whose family came from there."

"Yes. Carlos Santiago...you used to call him Charlie."

Zeke glanced at the file in front of Frank. "Pretty extensive study you made there. I suppose you have the name of the girl who stole my virginity noted, as well."

Frank glanced up from the papers and grinned. "I could probably make an educated guess."

Zeke rolled his eyes. "Never mind. So I was born in the lower part of the Rio Grande Valley. I suppose that would give me something of an advantage."

"Exactly. It would be logical and perfectly natural for you to return to Harlingen to regroup. De la Garza would be a natural prospect for a man of your talents."

"If the man is as smart as you say he is, I can't see him offering a job to someone who's worked for the U.S. government most of his adult life."

"By the time we embellish on your record, add a few shady exploits and plant a few charges, he'll know full well why you left and why you have no particular allegiance to our government. From his point of view you'd be a good man to have around."

Zeke stood and stretched, looking around the room once more before meeting Frank's inquiring gaze. He nodded, reaching for the stack of files.

"It sure beats tap dancing five times a day at Disney World."

One

Zeke casually leaned against a wall of the international airport in Mexico City, his hands in his pockets, and watched the trickle of people exiting the customs area.

Ignoring the speculative glances aimed in his direction by some of the women who passed, Zeke kept his gaze and thoughts focused on the passengers who had recently arrived from Madrid, Spain.

Although he had never seen her before, Zeke knew he would recognize Angela De la Garza. During the weeks he had been working for her uncle, Zeke had been in Lorenzo's office many times and had seen several photographs of the woman. He knew what she looked like as an infant in her mother's arms and what she looked like seated on the back of her prized pony when she was eight years old. He had seen her smiling face peering from multiple poses and situations spanning two decades.

Therefore, he would have no trouble recognizing the woman he had come to Mexico City to collect and fly back to Monterrey where she was to visit her uncle. He had no problem fulfilling the assignment. Taking orders from Lorenzo De la Garza was all part of his job, all strictly routine.

According to Lorenzo, Angela had a charming disposition. Too young when her parents died to remember much about them, she grew up considering Lorenzo to be her parent. He now admitted that he may have been too lax with her in an effort to make up for her loss. By the time he had placed her in a private school for her formal education, she had become quite self-willed and independent.

The nuns who taught Angela had reported her on numerous occasions...her lack of behavioral training had shocked them. She was continually being called in to the front office for talking too much in class, for laughing during study hours, and more often than not for failing to turn in completed homework.

Instead of improving when she entered high school, her actions incurred more frequent reprimands. Her hoydenish behavior often ran afoul of the rigid rules of the prim nuns. Lorenzo explained to Zeke that he finally had decided to send her to her mother's family in Spain during her second year in high school to finish her education, in hopes that they would be able to train her in the social graces expected from a properly brought-up young lady.

Lorenzo felt he had made the right decision. His beautiful, bright-eyed niece had matured into a warm,

vibrant woman with a great deal of charm. He had
made frequent visits to Madrid to see her during those
years. She had completed her education and had become an elementary school teacher, much to his surprise and pleasure. Lorenzo enjoyed talking about her
whenever he noticed Zeke looking at her photographs.

Consequently Zeke had become inordinately aware
of the young girl who stared back at him from all the
different poses. The latest one, taken in the spring
during Lorenzo's last visit, kept flashing into Zeke's
head at night when he closed his eyes to sleep.

The picture was an enlargement of a candid photograph taken out of doors near a waterfall and large
outcrop of rock. Green shoots of spring grass framed
her as she leaned against one of the boulders. The
spring green was reflected by the color of her eyes as
she gazed into the lens of the camera. Her hair was a
golden riot of waves streaked with shimmering strands
of copper and silver. The wind had tossed it into a
tousled mass of color that tumbled around her face
and shoulders.

She had been laughing into the camera, her face
glowing with love for whoever had taken the picture.
It was that expression that haunted his dreams at
night. During those late-night hours, she was looking
at *him* in just that way.

He'd never reacted so strongly to a woman before,
much less a photograph. Zeke enjoyed women. He
was attracted to those intelligent, self-confident ones
who were comfortable with who they were and didn't
feel the need for a special man in their lives to feel
complete.

In between assignments he generally spent his time with someone whose company he enjoyed. His women friends understood that their relationship created no binding commitments.

For him to be having fantasies about the niece of a man he hoped to bring down was the height of foolishness and he knew it. The fantasies hadn't become a problem until Lorenzo informed him that, despite everything he could say to discourage her, Angela was coming to visit him.

Zeke had known immediately that he had to wipe from his consciousness all of his fantasies now that the woman whose photograph had teased and tantalized him would soon be a part of his daily existence. He would distance himself from her emotionally, intentionally keeping a wall between them, and hope like hell that she would not be staying long.

At least Lorenzo joined him in that final wish, which helped. This was not a safe time to have a member of his family at the De la Garza compound, not after the recent trouble there.

The increasing tension surrounding De la Garza and his business had made Zeke's efforts to get hired by Lorenzo much easier than he or Frank could have planned. Zeke had been hired to beef up the security around the place and to serve as Lorenzo's personal bodyguard. The fact that he had lived in Europe for the past several years with no ties to the area caused Lorenzo to trust him more than he trusted some of the men he already had on his payroll.

Lorenzo knew he had a powerful enemy working hard to destroy him and his many businesses. He just didn't know who. Zeke assumed it was another cartel muscling in on Lorenzo's territory, but if Lorenzo had any suspicions about the identity of his enemy, he wasn't sharing them with anyone.

During the weeks he had worked for Lorenzo, Zeke had learned the layout of the place, met several of Lorenzo's business associates and had identified two undercover drug agents.

What he didn't know was which one was on the take. For that information he would need to get into Lorenzo's personal files in his office.

Lorenzo zealously guarded his office. He never allowed anyone inside when he wasn't there. The room was kept locked. Although locked doors had never been a problem for Zeke, he needed sufficient time to get inside and look through the files without being missed. However, since he rarely left Lorenzo's side, he'd yet to find the opportunity he needed.

Angela De la Garza had become an added nuisance in more than one respect. Not only did she already haunt his dreams, causing more than his fair share of sleepless nights, she would be one more person he had to elude before he could accomplish his assignment.

Zeke shifted his weight and propped his booted foot against the wall, his gaze focused on the incoming arrivals.

As soon as he spotted Angela, Zeke lazily pushed away from the wall and straightened to his full height. She looked smaller than he had expected. He wasn't a particularly large man, but he doubted that the top of her head came to his chin. She was also dressed more sedately than he'd pictured her. She wore a pale green suit and had her hair pulled away from her face in a formal style she had never worn for any of her uncle's photographs. The soft chignon would have been too severe for most women. For Angela, the style framed and emphasized the oval shape of her face and the creamy smoothness of her fair skin.

She bore little resemblance to her father's side of the family. Zeke recognized her resemblance to her mother in the pictures he had seen of her with Angela as a baby.

With a measured tread, Zeke moved toward the woman he had flown to Mexico City to meet, disguising his feelings behind an impassive mask.

Angie felt as though the air terminal were rocking like an ocean liner in a storm, but since no one else seemed to be affected by any unexplained movement she decided her reaction was due to the fatigue of her recent transatlantic flight. She had been unable to do more than nap on the plane during the flight. Now that she had arrived, she hoped that her excitement at seeing her uncle in a few minutes would give her a surge of energy that would carry her through the rest of the afternoon.

She hadn't been home in more than ten years. Despite Tio's repeated suggestions that she wait for a better time to visit, Angela had insisted that she didn't want to wait any longer. Every time she mentioned coming back home, he always had a list of reasons why she should delay her trip.

This time she had ignored him and come anyway. Would he forgive her for being so stubborn? Would he think that she was the same undisciplined person he had sent to Spain all those years ago?

Hopefully she would be able to quickly convince him that it was her love for him and for her home that had made her so insistent. Now that she was an adult he needn't worry so much about her. She could look after herself. She could be a help to him, as well.

Of course she was nervous about their initial meeting. How could she not be? But once he saw her, she knew he would forgive her for ignoring his suggestions about waiting to come visit him. He loved her. She knew that he would forgive her anything.

By the time she cleared customs, Angie had gotten a grip on her feelings. She was ready to face her uncle and—

A tall, broad-shouldered man coming toward her caught her attention, dispelling her reverie. He moved in an indolent stroll that emphasized the superb conditioning of his body. Her gaze was drawn to the subtle movement of his taut thigh muscles rippling beneath the fabric of his snug jeans. There wasn't an ounce of fat on the man.

She idly lifted her gaze to encompass his strong jawline, his unsmiling mouth, and a nose that looked to have been broken more than once. A bolt of shocked awareness struck her when she made eye contact with him. He'd been watching her while she mentally inventoried his physical assets!

Thoroughly embarrassed, Angie averted her gaze so that she was staring past him while she continued along the concourse.

"Miss De la Garza?"

The only thing more embarrassing than to be caught staring at a stranger was to have him speak your name. Angie knew she must be blushing and there wasn't a darned thing she could do about it.

His deep voice had touched a vibrating response from somewhere inside of her. She shivered, confused by her inexplicable reaction to a total stranger.

"Yes?" She paused in front of him, forcing herself to meet his dark-eyed gaze without betraying the swirl of emotions his appearance had provoked.

"My name is Zeke Daniels. I work for Lorenzo De la Garza. He sent me to meet your plane since he couldn't arrange his schedule to come, himself."

She looked around the busy area. "You mean my uncle isn't here?" she asked, suddenly feeling like a lost child who had not been claimed by her parents.

"That's right." He looked past her at the man who pushed a load of luggage on a dolly. "Are all of these yours?"

She stiffened. "Yes." Her gaze met his without flinching. "Do you have a problem with the amount of luggage I chose to bring with me?"

He shrugged. "Not really." He took her elbow. "We can grab a cab to take us over to the private hangar where your uncle's plane is being serviced."

She heard his words with dismay. She had hoped that Tio would agree to spend the night in Mexico City and give her a chance to rest before traveling any farther.

She glanced out one of the windows along the concourse at the dark clouds that had rapidly filled the sky. "But there's a storm moving in. Surely you aren't planning to fly in this weather?"

Zeke dropped her arm and placed his hands on his hips. "Look, lady, I'm just trying to do what I was told, okay? I'm not overjoyed by the prospect of flying through turbulent weather myself, but it wouldn't be the first time, and I doubt it will be the last."

Angie nibbled on her bottom lip and looked around her. She was overwhelmingly tired, so tired she felt as though she could sleep for a month without stirring.

She hadn't eaten much on the plane and was hungry.
Her uncle's nonappearance had hit her hard. She knew
he was not pleased with her, but to send a hired man
to pick her up as though she were unwanted freight
had pierced all her defenses.

Blindly she turned away from him and started down
the concourse alone. Zeke caught up with her in three
long strides and took her arm once again. She would
have walked into an oncoming couple if he hadn't
steered her deftly around them. Angie never noticed.

"Look, I can understand if you're afraid of flying
in a small plane in bad weather. I'm sure Lorenzo
would understand if we stay over. We'll go to one of
the hotels, check in and have an early dinner. How
does that sound?"

Another wave of dizziness swept over her and she
stumbled. Zeke slid his arm around her waist in alarm.
Her fair skin had turned a deathly white.

"Don't faint on me now, Princess," he muttered
under his breath. He guided her to one of the entrance doors, pushed it open, and waved at the near-
est taxi driver. While the driver and the baggage
handler began transferring her luggage to the trunk of
the taxi, Zeke eased Angie into the back seat.

She leaned her head against the seat and closed her
eyes with a sigh.

As soon as the luggage was stowed, Zeke gave the
driver the name of one of the luxury hotels, then
crawled in and sat beside Angie.

She opened her eyes. "Sorry for the wobbly knees.
I guess I'm just not used to traveling."

Zeke recognized the consequences of crossing several time zones in a short time. "Don't worry about
it...happens to everybody. I should have thought

about it myself and made plans to stay over. I'll call Lorenzo as soon as we get checked in."

What had happened to the wall he had intended to place between them? Seeing her so wan and vulnerable had wiped out all of his careful planning. Frowning, he looked away from her and stared at the passing scenery.

The silence that filled the cab for long minutes was interrupted by Angie's asking, "Did you say your name is Zeke?"

He looked around. "That's right."

She hadn't lifted her head from where it reclined against the seat. Her eyelids were puffy, making her look as though she had just woken up. Her sultry mouth drew his eyes, causing his body to react. Once again he looked away, this time clenching his jaw and reminding his body that *he* was the one in charge here and this woman was definitely off-limits.

His traitorous body ignored his lofty mental reprimands, and he found himself growing uncomfortable in his tight-fitting jeans.

"Are you a native of Mexico?"

He shifted restlessly. Still not looking at her, he replied, "No. I was born in South Texas."

"Ah. That explains why you speak Spanish like a native."

When he made no other response, she asked, "Have you worked for my uncle long?"

He shrugged. "A few weeks."

"Did he hire you as his pilot?"

Since his piloting skills had been part of his résumé, he could only guess at that one. "Among other things," he said.

"I'm eager to get back to the hacienda. Even though I've been gone so long, the mountains overlooking Monterrey have always seemed like home to me. I dream about them at times, thinking I'm back there. Then I wake up and discover that I'm still in Spain. I never knew how painful homesickness can be."

"I wouldn't know."

"I don't suppose you have that problem, living so close to where you were born. Do you visit there often?"

"No."

She waited, but he didn't add anything more.

They drew up in front of the hotel at the same time the low-hanging clouds dropped an avalanche of water upon the city. The doorman, prepared, hurried over to the taxi with a large umbrella.

Zeke got out first, then offered his hand to Angela. Her fingers felt small and delicate in his hand. As soon as was reasonably polite, he drew away from her, ostensibly to oversee the transfer of luggage, but more importantly to experience the driving force of the cold rain on his overheated body.

By the time he entered the hotel, Angela was already at the registration desk. When he walked up she turned to him, obviously upset. "They don't have any vacancies. They have two separate conventions booked and all the rooms are spoken for." Even as she spoke, her eyes widened. "Oh, Zeke, you're soaked."

The water had worked its cure, leaving its uncomfortable aftermath of wet clothing. He ruefully plucked at the front of the cotton shirt that was now plastered to his chest, pushed his hair away from his face and looked at the hotel employee behind the desk.

Reaching into his wallet, he pulled out a large-denomination bill, palmed it and rested his hand on the counter. Moving his hand slightly so the amount of the bill showed between his thumb and his forefinger, he said, "As you can see—" he glanced down at his clothes with resignation "—we really need a place to stay for the night. Would you mind checking again to see if you have *anything* available?"

Zeke wasn't too surprised a few minutes later when the clerk returned to say he had found a cancellation he had overlooked.

During their ride up in the elevator, Zeke tried to think of where he could find a shop to buy some clothes, since he hadn't brought any along on this trip. The bellman bringing their luggage held the door for them, then led them down a long hallway before pausing in front of one of the doors.

When the bellman stepped aside, Zeke followed Angela into what looked to be a sitting room. Open double doors revealed a large bedroom.

Zeke turned to the bellman. "I don't think the registration clerk understood that we need two rooms."

The bellman nodded. "Yes, sir. You're fortunate that this suite has not been claimed. This sofa—" he pointed "—makes out into a second bed. I'm afraid it's the best we can do under the circumstances."

"I'll sleep in here if you'd like the bedroom," Angela said quietly.

"Don't be ridiculous. Of course you can have the bedroom."

"There's another complete bath in here," the bellman said, opening a door off the sitting room. Then he pushed the cart of luggage into the bedroom and began to unload it.

Zeke turned to Angie, his frustration mounting. "I'm sorry, Miss De la Garza, I—"

"Please, it isn't your fault. And De la Garza is too formal. My friends call me Angie." She smiled at him. "I hope that we will become friends, Zeke."

Feeling trapped by circumstances over which he had no control, Zeke tipped the bellman and watched as he left the room, closing the door quietly behind him.

"You really should get out of those wet clothes, don't you think?" she asked after a moment.

Zeke growled, "Great idea. Hope you have something in one of those suitcases for me to wear because I neglected to bring a change of clothes on this little jaunt."

Angie nodded. "Actually, I do, if you don't mind going a little informal."

"Don't be silly. I couldn't possibly wear anything of yours."

"I was given a terry robe for my birthday, my girl-friend thought 'one size fits all' meant just that. Unfortunately, the robe swallowed me. I brought it, thinking I would give it to Tio. I'm sure it would fit you."

Zeke sneezed. He faced the fact that he didn't have a great many choices at the moment. The rain continued to beat against the windowpane. He sure as hell didn't feel like going shopping while in his wet clothes and the thought of getting dry appealed to him immensely.

Angie went into the bedroom and began to sort through her various bags. Opening one, she made a sound of satisfaction and brought him a forest-green terry-cloth robe. He almost smiled at its size. It would come very close to fitting him, which meant she would be lost in it.

"Thanks," he muttered, taking the robe and going into the bathroom.

He pulled off his boots before peeling off his wet jeans and draped the jeans across the counter to dry. Then he removed his shirt and did the same thing. Even his underwear and socks were damp. After he took off his socks and slid off his shorts, he turned on the shower.

The warm water caressed his chilled skin and he groaned with pleasure. He blanked out his mind to any thought other than the pleasure of that moment. Only when the water began to cool did he readjust it, then he picked up the soap and lazily washed himself.

He wasn't sorry that they weren't flying back today. He hadn't been pleased with the weather forecast when he had landed earlier and turned the plane over to the service department of the privately owned hangar. Perhaps it was just as well Angela had pushed him to delay their departure.

Angela. The familiar smiling photograph flashed into his mind to be slowly superimposed by a newer image, a more sedate, formal image of Angie.

"My friends call me Angie," she had said. "I hope that we will become friends, Zeke."

With another groan he turned off the water and grabbed a towel, vigorously drying himself. Maybe it *was* better that they weren't flying in this weather, maybe she *did* need a good night's rest before seeing Lorenzo again, but damn! why did they have to share the same suite?

He needed some distance from her, at least for a few hours. The last thing he needed was to be parading around in a bathrobe while she—

He didn't know what she would be doing, but he soon found out. When he came out of the bathroom, she was waiting for him in the sitting room, looking a little anxious.

"I, uh, hope you don't mind, but I would much prefer eating up here than having to go to a restaurant. So I called room service. I ordered their special for the evening, a seafood dish, for both of us. If you'd rather have something else—"

"No, I don't care what I have."

"I, uh, also called Tio to tell him about the storm and that I talked you into staying overnight. He wanted to speak with you and I explained that you were in the shower." She stopped and nibbled on her bottom lip. "Then I had to explain about the lack of space in the hotel at the moment."

Zeke leaned his shoulder against the doorjamb and crossed his arms over his chest. "I bet he was delighted to hear about that."

She shook her head. "Not really. He wants you to call him as soon as you're out of the shower."

"Somehow that doesn't surprise me."

"Our food should be here in another fifteen minutes or so. I'd like to shower and change before then."

"Don't let me stop you."

Her worried gaze met his. "I feel as though all of this—" she waved her hands at the room, at the rain beating at the windows "—is somehow my fault. Tio sounded upset and I didn't know what more to say."

"Go get your shower and stop worrying about it. You have no control over hotel conventions or the weather. Your uncle's just had a lot on his mind lately.''

''Sitting here, waiting for you to come out, I finally realized that my stubbornness has once again gotten me into trouble. I thought he would feel differently about my visit once I got here, but if anything, he sounds almost angry that I've inconvenienced him.''

Zeke straightened and moved over to where she sat on the edge of the couch. He leaned down and took her hand, pulling her up to stand beside him.

''Look, Angie. You're exhausted, that's all. When we get too tired, everything looks gloomy and nothing seems right. Don't let it color your judgment. I'm glad you ordered in.'' He glanced down at his robe. ''I'm certainly not dressed for a restaurant. Go ahead and take your shower. You'll feel better. Then we'll eat and you can get to bed early.''

She turned and walked out of the room and for a moment Zeke felt a strong need to wrap his arms around her and hold her for a long moment.

Instead, he picked up the phone and called his boss.

Two

"What the hell is going on?"

Zeke jerked the phone receiver away from his ear for a moment before responding to Lorenzo. "I was under the impression that Angie explained the circumstances to you."

"I want to know how you managed to arrange to spend the night in my niece's room, Daniels."

"I'm afraid I had nothing to do with the hotel accommodations. And I won't be spending the night in your niece's room, Lorenzo. There is a bedroom and a sitting room. In case Angie didn't mention it, the sofa in the sitting room makes out into a bed. I'm sure I'll be quite comfortable."

"I don't give a damn about your comfort. What I care about is my niece. What I care about is her reputation. Now why didn't you ignore her when she asked to stay overnight and get the hell back here?"

Once again Zeke stared out the window. The wind and the rain were still very much in evidence. "Look, Lorenzo, the forecast for this afternoon and evening was for heavy thunderstorms, which is the biggest reason I agreed to stay overnight when she suggested it. Angie didn't like the idea of flying in heavy weather. I saw no reason not to accommodate her. I didn't see any emergency about getting her home today under these circumstances. The storm should be gone by morning. The weather bureau is predicting clear skies and sunny weather for tomorrow. There was no need to take unnecessary risks."

"I don't like it."

"You don't like what?"

"Your staying there together."

Zeke sighed. "All right. I'll find another hotel to stay in. Will that make you feel better?"

"Considerably."

"Anything else?"

"Yes. We found an intruder on the grounds today. That new surveillance equipment you suggested paid off. We wouldn't have known he got over the wall, otherwise."

"Glad to be of service. Did you find out what he was doing there?"

"Not yet, but I intend to. When do you expect to get here tomorrow?"

"We should be there by noon. If you like, I'll deal with the man and see what I can find out for you."

"What I want to know is who's behind this rash of break-ins and other problems. I'm sick to death of living under siege against an enemy I can't identify."

"I'm working on that. If you had sent someone else to pick up your niece, I would still be there working on it."

"I know, I know. But my other pilot doesn't have your experience. I wanted to know that Angela was safe. I thought you were the man for the job."

"I'm trying to be, believe me."

"Okay, okay. Maybe I'm just being jumpy. I wish to hell Angela could have picked another time to come."

"I'm aware of that. You've voiced your concern on many occasions."

"Tell her I'm sorry I yelled at her."

Zeke grinned. "I'm sure that will make her feel much better."

"I've been under a strain."

"I'll tell her."

"No! Don't tell her about the strain. She doesn't need to know anything about what's been going on. Just apologize for me for being in a temper."

"I'll do that," Zeke responded dryly.

"I'll see you tomorrow," Lorenzo said, and hung up.

Zeke hung up the phone, shaking his head. Then he dialed housekeeping and asked them to send someone to pick up his clothes. He had to have them dry before he could go looking for another place to stay.

There was a tap on the door and a voice announced, "Room service." He tightened the sash of his robe and went over to the door. After viewing the hall through the security opening, Zeke opened the door and waved the hotel employee inside.

The serving cart was set for two people, and the setting included a perfectly formed red rosebud in a cut crystal vase. Zeke signed the charge ticket for the meal, tipped the waiter and closed the door behind him.

Everything was ready, even to a carafe of coffee. Silently thanking Angie for her thoughtfulness, he poured a cup of coffee and sat on the sofa to wait for her.

When she walked through the door and saw him, she blushed. "I hope you don't mind, but I, uh—well, I didn't really want to get dressed again." She glanced down at the silk pajamas and matching robe. "I thought I'd get ready for bed."

Zeke stood, thankful for the concealing folds of his robe. Damn, but she looked adorable standing there with her hair loose around her shoulders. Now she looked like the photograph that haunted his dreams. "You should always wear your hair down like that," he heard himself saying, appalled by his lack of discretion.

Her blush deepened and he could have kicked himself for causing her to be more uncomfortable with their circumstances. He motioned to the table.

"Don't worry about your appearance. Let's eat so that you can get some rest." He pulled out a chair and motioned for her to sit down. There was a knock at the door.

"I'll be right back," he said, striding across the room.

"But who—"

After making sure who was there, he opened the door to a woman who explained she was from housekeeping. He stepped into the bathroom, gathered up his wet clothes, came out and handed them to her with a tip. "Thank you for being so prompt. I'd like to have these back as soon as possible."

She bobbed her head and left.

Zeke returned to the table.

Angie watched him as he sat down and picked up his fork. "I wonder what that woman thought of us in our robes this early in the evening."

Zeke grinned. "Probably thinks we're honeymooners." He almost laughed at her deepened color as she picked up her salad fork, studying it intently, as though fascinated by the pattern.

After a moment, he asked, "Do you really care what she thinks?"

Angie glanced up and became aware of him watching her. "Tio was upset about our sharing a room," she said.

"Yeah. He told me. As soon as my clothes come back I'm going to look for a room in another hotel."

"But there's no need for you to do that!" As though realizing that he might misinterpret her meaning, she explained, "I mean, there's plenty of room here, if you don't mind sleeping on the sofa. Tio is being ridiculous." She took a bite of her salad.

"Is he?"

She picked up her glass and took a sip of water. "Well, of course. There's no reason to think—" She seemed to bog down in that line of reasoning.

"I take it you trust me not to attack you sometime during the night."

"How silly! Why would you do something like that?"

He thought about her comment while he polished off his salad. After retrieving their entrées from the warming oven of the serving cart, he asked, "How old did you say you are?"

Startled, she replied, "I haven't said. Why do you ask?"

"Either you've lived an extremely sheltered life and know absolutely nothing about men," he drawled, "or—" He took a bite of his dinner, chewed it very carefully, swallowed, then continued "—you have absolutely no idea how desirable you are."

She dropped her fork onto her plate and placed her hands in her lap. "You're making fun of me."

That was the last reaction he expected.

"Not at all. Actually, I'm paying you a rather crude compliment. But at least it's sincere." He studied her while he continued to eat. Hesitantly she resumed eating, as well.

"Have you known many men while you were growing up?" Now he really was curious about her.

She shook her head. "Not really, other than relatives, of course. I've always attended private girls' schools. I teach in a coeducational school, and there are a few male teachers, but I don't see them outside of school functions."

"You don't date?"

She shook her head.

"Why not?"

"Because not many have asked me. Those that have I wasn't interested in. Besides, my family frowned on my going out with a man alone."

"You're kidding. Do they still have chaperons?"

"Sometimes. But it isn't that. I have always planned to come back to Mexico. I knew that if I were to get involved with someone living in Spain there was a good chance I would never return home."

"So you've led a very sheltered life and have no idea just how beautiful you are."

Her cheeks lit up like a neon sign.

"Hey, I didn't mean to embarrass you. Really. Think of me as another uncle, one who's too outspoken. Ignore me."

She smiled, but the smile didn't hide her fatigue and he felt like a heel for baiting her.

"If you're through eating, why don't you go to bed?"

"It wouldn't be very polite of me to—"

"Forget polite. You can be as polite to me as you wish tomorrow. I'll wait here for my clothes, then I'll slip out. I'll give you a call in the morning in time to get an early start. How's that sound?"

They both stood, then she held out her hand to him. When he took it, she said, "You've been very kind to me, Zeke. I know I've been a nuisance. Thank you for your patience."

"Hey, the last thing I am is a kind person. You must be more tired than I thought." He rubbed his thumb over the back of her hand, feeling the delicate bones. Without thought, he brought her hand up to his mouth, turned it and placed a kiss in her palm. "Pleasant dreams, Princess," he murmured, releasing her hand.

She stood there staring at him, her eyes wide. This close he could see the different shades of green in their depths. He also saw the dark smudges of fatigue beneath her eyes.

Angie turned and went into the bedroom, closing the double doors behind her. He pushed the serving cart into the hallway, then walked over to the window and looked out. The rain appeared to be lessening, which was a good sign. Hopefully by tomorrow they would have clear skies.

He glanced over at the sofa. He might as well stretch out and get comfortable, maybe take a nap, while he was waiting for his clothes. Then, like an obedient employee, he'd go find himself a room for the night.

Angie crawled into bed, sighing with relief to be able to lie down after countless hours of travel. She snuggled into her pillow, anticipating oblivion for the next few hours.

Instead, her mind raced—playing back the last few hours, leaping ahead to her meeting with Tio, flashing images of Zeke Daniels.

Once again she experienced her disappointment that Tio hadn't met her plane. There was so much she wanted to tell him in person. Now she would have to wait another day before she found out his reaction to her plans. She'd allowed him to believe she was coming to visit when she fully intended to stay. Mexico was her home. She had spent years getting her education so that she could return to Mexico. Her dream was to start a preschool in one of the mountain villages near Tio's place.

She'd been afraid to tell him before because he seemed to discourage any discussion of her returning home. Now that she was here, she intended to show him that she had overcome her impulsive nature and could behave as a responsible adult.

Her mind slowed and her thoughts drifted. An image of Zeke Daniels appeared. She was curious about him, more curious than she'd ever been about a man before. He had an embarrassingly strong effect on her, one she didn't understand. Being around him made

her blood race and caused her to stammer in confusion. Never before had she been so aware of a man.

What was it about him that so unnerved her?

He was so self-assured, even in a borrowed bathrobe. He made her aware of her own femininity, of the
differences between his strong, muscular strength and
her own softness.

He intrigued her. She wanted to get to know him
better. Since he worked for Tio, she shouldn't have
much difficulty.

She sighed, drifting into sleep, a smile on her face.

Hours later Zeke came awake with a start. The lamp
cast a dim glow in the room. He sat up, glancing at his
watch. It was after two o'clock in the morning.

He went to the door and checked the hallway. The
room service cart was gone, but there was no sign of
his clothes. He should have been more specific about
when he needed them, but he had thought "as soon as
possible" was clear enough.

He had little option other than to stay there. He
certainly couldn't go anywhere in a bathrobe. He returned to the sofa and, this time, pulled out the bed
and turned back the sheets. After searching for a pillow, he found one in the closet, then, discarding his
robe, crawled into bed with a sigh. He turned out the
light and closed his eyes, willing himself to sleep once
more.

Sometime later a soft tap on the door awakened
him. The room lay in the quiet early light of day-
break. Zeke pulled on the robe and went to the door.

"Who is it?"

"Laundry."

He peeked through the door, recognized his freshly laundered clothes on a hanger and opened the door.

"We also have a complimentary toiletry kit in case you needed one," the young man said.

"Thanks." Zeke signed for the delivery, pleased to spot a razor, comb and toothbrush in the small bag.

He headed for the bathroom, ready to get on with the day.

Once dressed, Zeke went over to the bedroom door and rapped. After a lengthy pause during which there was no sound, he eased open the door and peeked inside.

Angie lay sprawled across the bed on her stomach, her face almost obscured by a pillow. One knee was bent, causing the thin pajama material to snugly mold the curve of her bottom. The pajama top had ridden up, exposing a fair amount of her bare back. Her hair lay in a tangle of curls across the pillow, spilling down across her shoulders.

An unexpected jolt of sharp desire shot through him, causing his body to immediately respond to the enticing picture she made.

Zeke stepped back and hastily closed the door. Opening that door had not been one of his better ideas. He should have known she was still asleep. He should have known—never mind. He would call her from downstairs in accordance with the original plan. As far as she knew he had not spent the night there.

He returned the sofa to its original state, folded the bathrobe and left it lying on the arm of one of the chairs. Then he slipped silently out of the room.

Angie knew there was something she needed to do, something that kept tugging at her, but she was too relaxed and comfortable to move. If whoever or whatever it was would just go away she would continue to drift and to dream.... But the noise continued until she surfaced enough from her deep sleep to recognize the annoying sound was the telephone busily ringing only a few feet from her head.

Groaning, she rolled over and groped for the noisy instrument. "H'lo?" she mumbled.

A deep voice growled seductively into her ear. "C'mon, sleepyhead. It's time to rise and shine. I'll meet you downstairs for breakfast in half an hour."

The caller hung up before she could manage a reply.

Still more than half-asleep, she fumbled with the receiver until she could replace it on its base. With her eyes still closed, she thought about what she had just heard.

Breakfast. Half hour. Rise and shine.

She forced one eye open and stared at the bedside clock. It lacked a couple of minutes to seven o'clock. How could that be when she had gone to bed only a few minutes ago? She reluctantly sat up and stared around her. The room was unfamiliar and she felt as though she had a severe hangover. Where was she and what had she been doing?

Bits and pieces of the previous day ran across her mind like a silent movie. She remembered a pair of piercing dark eyes staring at her... her disappointment that Tio hadn't been at the airport to meet her... a hauntingly deep voice suggesting—

Suggesting breakfast! Oh, dear. Zeke would be downstairs waiting on her if she didn't hurry. Tossing the covers to the side, she climbed out of bed and hurried to the bathroom.

Her dreams had been a jumble of impressions, but she distinctly remembered seeing those eyes staring at her and feeling the tingling kiss he had placed in her palm.

She would see him in a half hour. Angie realized her heart was racing with a mixture of agitation and anticipation at being in Zeke's company once again.

She saw him as soon as she stepped off the elevators, her eyes drawn inexorably toward his tall, lean figure. She didn't understand what it was about him that drew the eye, but she noticed that she wasn't the only one who noticed the man leaning against one of the pillars in the lobby with his arms folded across his chest.

"Good morning," she said, wishing she didn't sound quite so breathless. "You're looking well rested this morning. Did you have any trouble finding a place to sleep?"

His lopsided grin appeared. "Not at all," he answered in complete honesty. "How about you? Did you sleep all right?" He took her by the elbow and guided her into the coffee shop.

"I must have. I can't believe I slept for almost twelve hours!"

She looked dazzling in the morning sunlight. Zeke was having trouble concentrating on what she was saying. He had known as soon as she stepped off the elevator that he was in a heap of trouble.

Her colorful silk blouse and tailored skirt were probably not considered provocative attire, but they set off the gentle curves that he had dreamed about most of the night. Like it or not, she was a distraction that he was having difficulty overcoming, and his life depended on his not becoming distracted.

As soon as the waiter took their order, Zeke searched for a neutral topic. "I guess you're looking forward to getting home today."

"Yes, but I might as well admit that I'm not looking forward to the flight." She sighed. "Small planes have always frightened me."

He settled back in his chair and said, "Or is it the pilot you don't trust?"

Her eyes widened. "Oh, no! I'm sure you're very competent or my uncle would never have hired you."

"Well, I'll try to make the flight as pleasant for you as possible."

Zeke was thankful when their breakfast arrived and he didn't have to concern himself with further conversation. They only had a few more hours together. He could handle that with no problem.

Probably by the time they reached Monterrey he would be eager to be rid of the woman. Being around her these extra hours would no doubt wipe out all those fantasies he'd created, using her image.

He could only hope.

Three

Angie sat beside Zeke in the cockpit of her uncle's plane, listening and watching as he spoke to the control tower through his headset while they waited for their signal to take off.

Now that they were ready to take off the butterflies that had taken up permanent residence in her stomach had multiplied and were busy giving flying instructions to their many young. Was their feverish activity due to her fear of flying in a small plane, her nervousness about facing her uncle, or her awareness of Zeke sitting so closely beside her she could easily rest her hand on his muscled thigh?

Perhaps her butterflies were the result of all three conditions.

Zeke motioned for her to put on the headset lying in front of her. As soon as she had it on, she heard the crackling of static and a disembodied voice giving them clearance. Zeke taxied the plane to the end of the runway, saying, "It will be easier to communicate if you'll keep the headset on." She nodded, wondering what he thought they would be communicating about.

She thought she had masked her nervousness. Had he thought she would panic? If so, being tuned in to control tower conversation was not going to help her in the slightest.

The noise all around her intensified and the plane started quivering like a racehorse eager to hear the opening gun. At an incomprehensible—to Angie—signal over the headphones, Zeke gave the plane its head and it leaped forward, moving down the runway at an ever-increasing speed.

Angie had never ridden in the cockpit of a plane before. Seeing the ground rush toward her faster and faster made her catch her breath and forget to breathe. As the runway quickly shortened, she closed her eyes, feverishly praying beneath her breath that the plane would lift off the ground in time.

She wasn't certain how much time passed before Zeke said, "You can open your eyes now," in a dry voice.

Reluctantly she forced her eyes open, feeling humiliated by her cowardice. She braced herself for his open derision but discovered, when she looked his way, that he was busy comparing the terrain against an open map in front of him.

"We should have a smooth flight," he went on, as though continuing a conversation they had been having. "The early morning good weather looks to be holding. The only bumpy areas are over the mountains, and that can't be helped."

"What do you mean?"

"The air drafts over the mountains are inconsistent at the altitude we're flying. I'll try to give you some warning before we're affected."

She glanced out and down, her eyes widening at the sight. "Why, it's beautiful from here."

"Yes, it is."

"I had no idea. There's a much better view in a smaller plane."

He gave a lopsided smile without looking at her. "That has its good points, as well as its bad."

"I'm sorry for being so frightened. It really isn't scary at all."

"Hey, lady. You don't owe me any apologies. Sometimes I forget what it's like to fly when you're not accustomed to it."

"How long have you been flying?"

"More years than I can remember."

"Do you enjoy it?"

"Never gave the idea much thought. Flying gets me where I need to go faster than any other method I've found."

"How did you learn?"

Zeke realized that she still wasn't over her nervousness. He hadn't planned to give her the story of his life. Then again, maybe he could lull her to sleep with some of the dull details.

"The U.S. government taught me. I was in the air force."

"Oh. When was that?"

"I joined as soon as I graduated from college. Not one of my wiser moves, but it seemed the thing to do at the time."

"Did you stay in the air force long?"

"Six years. Then I found out I could make more money using my skills in civilian life."

"Doing what?"

"I joined an outfit that worked mostly overseas. I spent the next several years learning just how green I was."

She was quiet for a few moments before she asked, "What did your family think about your working so far away?"

"My mother died my senior year at college. My dad remarried and ended up raising his new wife's three children. He didn't have much time to be concerned about me."

"Do you see them very often?"

"No. I doubt I'd recognize any of the children if I were to run into them."

"That's sad."

"What's sad about it?"

"That you aren't close to your family. I've missed having parents and brothers and sisters. Tio has been wonderful to me and I would never hurt his feelings by complaining, but a child alone can become very lonely."

His gaze routinely checked the instrument panel, paused, then swept back to one of the gauges. The oil pressure was dropping. He didn't like the looks of that.

"Tio was so good to me. When I was smaller he used to take me with him on his business trips. We would inspect factories, discuss wool grading, talk to manufacturers. He never made me feel that I was in his way, or that he was sorry he brought me along with him. He—"

"Angie, I don't mean to interrupt, but—"

"What is it? What's wrong?" There was something strange in his voice... carefully neutral, as though...

"I think we're going to have to make a stop before we get to your uncle's place."

She stared out at the landscape. They were over rolling hills that were rapidly becoming a mountain range.

"Where? There's no airport around, is there?"

He reached for the radio and began to give their call letters, asking for assistance.

There was no response.

He muttered something beneath his breath that she felt was just as well she hadn't heard.

She lightly touched his arm and felt the tension there. "What's wrong? Are we out of gasoline?"

"Just as bad. It looks as though we're losing oil... and fast. I'm going to have to put her down. Maybe I'll spot a road. Help me look, would you?"

During the next tense moments, the silence seemed to grow and expand. All Angie could hear was the reassuringly steady sound of the single engine droning away.

"There!" She pointed off to her side of the plane to a brown snakelike path on the side of a mountain. "Do you see it?"

He nodded and banked the plane, decreasing their altitude as he headed in the new direction.

"It's awfully twisty, isn't it?" she breathed.

"Honey, at this point we don't have much choice. Just hang on. I promise I'll get you down in one piece. I never make a promise I can't keep, okay? You're going to be just fine."

For some reason that she didn't understand, her earlier nervousness disappeared. Angie had no way of knowing whether the stranger beside her could keep his promise to her, but she discovered that she trusted him. If there was a way to land safely, this man would accomplish it.

She watched the hills and heavily wooded area rushing toward them as they dropped their speed and altitude. Her eerie calm continued to hold. She watched as though she were an observer to the action rather than a participant, as though the outcome of their forced landing did not truly affect her.

As the land continued to expand in an upwardly growing movement, she could pick out details—she saw individual trees instead of a blur of green color... the road, still winding, seemed to widen and grow in width and length... boulders took three-dimensional shape.

Angie felt it was important for her to continue to face what was happening to them. She didn't want to close her eyes and wait for whatever was going to happen to her... to them... when they attempted a landing.

Zeke knew what he needed for a runway length to land. He also knew the wing clearance that was mandatory if they were to survive the next few minutes. His eyes quickly scanned the area below him, intent on finding what he needed in the short time he had left. His choices were limited.

He had been in tight places before, but he'd never had a plane go out on him before. He was too careful, going over each one carefully. There had been no warning on the flight south yesterday. There had been nothing in the preflight check earlier to point to a problem with the oil line.

None of that mattered now. What he had to do was to get them down on the ground with as little damage as possible to either the plane or to them.

The plane began to sputter and he knew his options were gone. "Lean down! Put your face on your knees," he shouted without looking at the woman beside him. He didn't have time to make sure she had followed his instructions as he dropped the flaps and pushed the stick forward.

They hit hard...which wasn't surprising considering the rough texture of the road. The plane bucked like an untamed horse after its first taste of a bridle. Grimly Zeke hung on, muttering, not sure if he was praying or cursing.

He saw a tree close to the road and sharply cut the wheel, hoping to miss it. The sudden swerve of the tires caught a rut, causing the plane to tilt slightly.

He continued to fight for control, but it was too late. The tip of the wing came into contact with something, causing the plane to canter and the cockpit to spin.

The last he remembered was cutting off the engine before the screen of trees seemed to rise up in front of him, covering him in darkness.

Angela became aware of how quiet it was after the engine stopped and they had quit moving. Shakily she raised her head and looked around.

They were at a sharp angle, facing a thick line of trees a few feet in front of them. She turned and looked at Zeke, who was slumped over the wheel.

Tentatively she touched his shoulder. "Zeke? Are you all right?"

His lack of response frightened her more than anything that had happened. Didn't they need to get out of the plane? Wasn't there a fear of fuel leakage and possible fire whenever a plane crashed?

"Zeke?"

She released her breath when he groaned and attempted to straighten. He let out a hissing sound, then slowly forced himself upright in the seat. Carefully he turned his head and looked at her. Blood ran from a cut on his forehead. Awkwardly he lifted his right hand and touched the wound on the left side of his face.

"You okay?" he asked, a muscle in his jaw jumping with tension. He had his teeth clenched.

She nodded. "But you aren't. You're bleeding!" she said, her voice shaking.

He nodded. "Can you reach the first aid box behind you? There should be some pads in there."

She fumbled with the straps that had held her so securely in place, then found the box. Opening it, she removed some pads and bandages, which she tore free of their wrappings. She leaned over and held the pad against his head.

That's when she saw his shoulder. There was something wrong, but she couldn't tell exactly what. "What's wrong with your shoulder?"

"I think it's dislocated, but I'm not sure. I just know it hurts like the very devil." He shifted in an attempt to take the weight off his left arm, which had been thrown against the side of the plane when they hit.

Angie had to brace herself to keep from toppling over on him. After hurriedly tying a strip of gauze around Zeke's head to keep the pad in place, she undid the straps around him and with his help eased him out of the seat. Because the left wing was crumpled and the door jammed, they had to crawl out of the plane at an upward angle.

Once on the ground, Zeke surveyed the damage. The left wing was finished and the wheel on that side had been broken off. Outside of that, the fuselage and the tail structure appeared intact.

Zeke checked the gas tank, relieved not to find a rupture there. He moved toward Angie, keeping a tight grip on his left arm in an effort to keep the weight from causing the throbbing pain to increase to fiery flames of intense agony. He stopped in front of her while she eyed him uncertainly.

"Will you help me get my shirt off? If we can rig a sling for my arm, I won't need to use my other arm for support."

He fumbled with the buttons until she nudged his hand aside and quickly unfastened the shirt. He held out his good arm. She tugged on the sleeve until he could slip his arm out, then she went up on her toes to slide it off his shoulders. In doing so, she found her nose almost buried in his warm chest.

Angie had never been so close to a shirtless man before. She was intensely aware of the hard planes, as well as the thick mat of curls that covered the broad expanse.

She took a step back, drew an unsteady breath and eased the shirt over his injured shoulder and arm, aware of the hiss of pain that escaped from his clenched teeth.

"I'm sorry," she whispered contritely. Never had Angie felt so inadequate in a situation. Zeke was the one injured and he was having to tell her what to do. She folded the shirt and slipped it around his arm. "If you can lean down toward me, I'll tie it behind your back."

Now that his adrenaline level had dropped a little, Zeke could feel the excruciating pain in his shoulder even more. His head burned where he'd received the cut. He leaned against the wing of the plane and allowed Angie to tie his shirt for him. He hoped the bone in his shoulder wasn't broken. He had enough problems without that at the moment.

"There. That should hold," he heard her say.

Zeke opened his eyes and stared into a pair of worried green ones only inches away. "Thanks."

"I'm sure it hurts quite dreadfully."

He sighed. "Yeah, well, you know how us macho types are . . . we can't admit to feeling minor pain."

She ignored his attempt at humor. "I've got something for pain in my purse, if you think it will help. I need it every month when I— That is, I'm sure it would help you just as much, if you'd like to try some."

He closed his eyes for a brief moment, considering. When he opened them, he said, "Sounds good to me, even if it shoots my image all to hell."

She found her purse and the small vial inside, then returned to the plane for the thermos that Zeke had filled with water before they left Mexico City. After carefully pouring the clear liquid into the lid, she placed two tablets in his mouth and held the container for him.

She shivered at the touch of his breath on her fingers, feeling foolish at her reaction. Why this man should make her feel so nervous, she wasn't certain. Why he affected her heart and breathing rate whenever she got this close to him was an even bigger mystery.

He took the thermos lid from her quivering fingers and drained the water from it. "Thanks." He looked at the road that turned out of sight only a few yards ahead of them. "At least we made it down in one piece."

"Yes. You did a magnificent job of landing safely."

He started toward the front of the aircraft. "I've got to see what happened to our oil pressure."

"Do you think you should be moving around just yet? Maybe if you rest for a while—"

Zeke cut his eyes around at her from where he stood by the cowl of the engine. "I'll let you know if I need any more help, okay?"

Angie nodded, silenced by his look more than his words. She watched as he lifted the cowl and began to check out the mysterious intricacies of the engine.

Glancing around them, she saw nothing but trees, boulders and the deserted road. "If there were any people nearby they would surely have heard us come down," she said into the silence.

"That's true enough," he replied without looking up from what he was doing. After several more minutes of silence he let out a muffled oath, drawing her attention back to him.

"What's wrong?"

"Someone cut through the oil line."

A tiny wisp of fear wended its way through her stomach. Walking over to where he stood, she paused to clear her throat before asking, "Are you sure?"

He straightened and looked around at her. "I'm sure. Whoever did it had the cut line spliced so that only after the oil got hot would the splice melt away, letting the oil leak out."

He'd gotten some oil on his hand and on one of his bare shoulders. Her gaze kept returning to his chest. She forced herself to look away, staring at the trees and the sharp incline of the road.

"What are we going to do?"

He looked around the deserted area, as well. "Good question."

"Who would want to cause us engine problems?"

"Another good question. I have a hunch they wanted to cause more than engine problems. We could have easily crashed once the oil was gone and the engine overheated."

The wisp of fear seemed to grow and wrap around her. She shivered, hugging her elbows. In an attempt to lighten the situation, she asked, "Do you by any chance have an enemy or two you neglected to mention?"

He eyed her warily. "Maybe. Maybe not. Maybe it was someone who didn't want *you* to reach home."

When he saw the look on her face, he wished he hadn't been so quick to respond to her teasing. However, the facts were obvious. Somebody had decided to get rid of one—or both—of them. Whoever it was had somehow managed to breach the hangar security where he had left the plane the night before. Or maybe it was one of the employees there. Had they been bribed?

Who would want to have him—or Angie—killed?

Was it possible someone had discovered what he was doing in Mexico and had decided to use this opportunity to silence him?

Zeke carefully wiped his fingers on an oil rag, wincing at the movement of his arm, then walked over to where Angela stood in the middle of the road.

He could feel the beads of perspiration trickle down his back from the heat of the overhead sun. He also knew that once the sun set the air would cool rapidly.

He looked up and down the deserted roadway. "Well, whoever they are, they're going to be powerfully disappointed, aren't they?" He ducked under the wing and stepped up so that he could crawl into the cockpit. He discovered a couple of flying jackets, a towel and more first aid supplies.

He gathered up the flight maps and other items, stuffing them into a small duffel bag, then got out of the plane.

"Did you happen to notice any villages or settlements earlier?" he asked, unfolding one of the maps.

"No."

"Neither did I, although I wasn't concentrating on anything but a landing strip at the time." He studied the topographical map for long, silent minutes. He could see why his request for assistance had gone unanswered. There was very little in the way of civilization along this stretch of the mountains. They were about halfway between Mexico City and Monterrey.

The question now was, what would be the best direction for them to take in order to find help quickly? It was anybody's guess.

He glanced around at the woman standing there watching him. She had regained some color in her face, probably due to the heat. Her hair had come out of its neat coil. Feathery wisps hung around her ears and neck and across her forehead.

She wasn't dressed for wilderness survival, there was no doubt about that. In her neatly tailored blouse and skirt, she looked totally out of place standing on that dusty and deserted road.

From all indications, they weren't going to get any immediate help from nearby residents. That didn't leave them with very many options. "This road must lead somewhere," he said, wiping a trickle of perspiration from his cheek. He glanced down at the duffel bag at his feet. "I'm going to go look for some help, maybe a ride into the closest town, something." He turned to her. "Do you want to wait with the plane or come with me?"

She looked up and down the road, looked at the plane, then finally met his gaze. "Are you going to leave the plane sitting here blocking the road?"

His head was pounding, the bright sunlight hurt his eyes, and the heat was making him feel nauseous. At the moment he didn't really care what happened to the damned plane.

"Are you afraid we're going to cause a traffic jam?"

She didn't say anything to that, but she felt uncomfortable with the idea of abandoning the plane. However, she liked the idea of staying there alone even less. She glanced down at her clothes, thankful for her low-heeled shoes.

She wasn't sure what she should do. Shouldn't one of them stay with the plane in case they were spotted from the air? But if Zeke was determined to go looking for help, did she dare allow him to go alone?

He could be more seriously injured than he was letting on. What if he barely got out of sight before he passed out? She would be sitting there alone, waiting for help that would never come, while he would be unconscious, a prey to whatever wild animals might live in these mountains.

She shivered at the thought. Why did she have to have such a vivid imagination?

"I'll go with you," she said. "Do you have any idea how long it will take to find someone?"

"In the best of all possible worlds, we'll find a Texaco station around the next bend, but somehow I don't think that's going to happen." He motioned to the plane. "Do you want anything out of your luggage before we go? I can't guarantee that whatever you leave will be here when we return, although I intend to lock it."

She crawled into the plane and opened her bags, staring into them. She was thankful she'd carried a large handbag. At least she could put her smaller necessities in there.

Once she was out of the plane with her clothes, she added them to the items in the duffel bag. Zeke locked the plane and said, "I think we'll head in that direction." He pointed toward the mountains. "Since we didn't see anything as we were flying over, we can only hope there's something up ahead." They started down the road.

Angie didn't give much thought on what was up ahead of them. She was too concerned about Zeke. With his head bandaged and his arm in a sling, he looked like a wounded warrior walking beside her. She tried to keep her concern from him but noticed that he made no effort to move faster than the pace she set.

By the time the sun began to set several hours later, she was hard-pressed not to panic. They hadn't seen a soul, nor had there been any traces of people living nearby.

The side of Zeke's face was swollen and discolored and he was holding his body stiff, as though every jolting step shot through him with agonizing regularity.

They were going to have to find a place to spend the night before the light was gone. She kept glancing at Zeke. He hadn't said anything for more than an hour. She had offered to carry the small duffel bag shortly after they started walking, but he had refused and she hadn't pushed the issue.

Her eyes searched the horizon as she had been doing repeatedly for hours. Only this time she saw a wisp of smoke in the distance.

Four

***

"Zeke! Look over there!"

The heat and the continued jarring of his shoulder with every step he took had done nothing to improve Zeke's pain these past several hours. He had been forcing himself to keep moving, concentrating on placing first one foot, then the other, in front of him.

Left, right, left, right. Reminded him of the military, always marching somewhere, always—

Angie tugged on his arm, breaking his concentration.

"There's smoke coming from the other side of that hill. Perhaps there's a settlement over there."

Zeke stared in the direction she was pointing, forcing his eyes to focus. After a moment he saw smoke slowly rising above the tops of the trees.

He stopped and absently rubbed his head.

"Is your head bothering you?"

"A little. That and my shoulder. The pain certainly hasn't gone away."

"Do you want to take another one of my pain relievers?"

He was tempted, definitely tempted. Then he looked around them, surprised to see how far the sun had moved along its arc in the sky. Glancing back at the smoke, he said, "Let's check out the smoke. Maybe we can find a phone or a car or something. I'm afraid if I take anything for pain now, I'll fall asleep."

Zeke led the way through the trees, heading directly for the crest of the hill. By the time they reached the top, they were both breathing hard.

They saw a primitive log cabin nestled in a small clearing below them. The smoke was drifting upward from a stone chimney.

"Well, at least we found a place where we can stay," Angie pointed out, trying to find something positive to say. "And we know someone's there." She glanced up at Zeke, worried about his lack of color. "You need to rest. Let's go let them know we're here."

They were lucky to have spotted anyone living in these mountains, Zeke decided, concentrating on taking each step. Those who had chosen to live among the mountains were reclusive by nature and wouldn't appreciate being disturbed by outsiders. He would have to make them understand about the plane...make them understand...what was happening to the light? The sun was going down too quickly. They were running out of light. Thank God, they were almost at the cabin....

Zeke stumbled and, instead of catching himself, slid to the ground in a boneless heap. Angie grabbed his uninjured arm but couldn't keep him from going down.

"Zeke!"

Angie looked around, wondering what to do. He was too heavy for her to move. Turning toward the cabin, she trotted up to the door and knocked. When no one answered, she knocked again, saying, "Please, can you help us? Our plane went down and the pilot is injured. Please. Won't you help us?"

After agonizing minutes that seemed to stretch into hours, the door slowly swung inward. An elderly woman stood there, looking uneasy.

"Oh, thank you," Angie said as soon as the door opened. "Is there someone who could help me move him inside?" She motioned to where Zeke lay, unconscious. "We've been walking for several hours and he's been in considerable pain." She glanced back at Zeke. "I don't know what to do for him."

The woman stepped out of the cabin with dignified grace. "I'm alone here, but I will see what I can do." She quickly headed toward Zeke. "What are his injuries?"

Angie kept up with the woman's rapid pace. "I think his shoulder is the worst, plus he has a cut on his head."

"How long ago did this happen?"

"Sometime this morning. I don't know how long that's been."

They reached Zeke and knelt beside him. The woman eased the head bandage off and looked at the wound, then lightly touched his shoulder. He moaned without regaining consciousness.

"His shoulder is dislocated. We mustn't leave it like this. The longer the shoulder is out, the more difficulty he will have." She motioned to Angie. "Come. You must help me."

Angie had been watching the woman's competent movements with a sense of bewilderment. "How do you know what to do?" she asked.

The woman glanced up. "I was a nurse for many years in a hospital near the coast. I'm too old to work, but I haven't lost the knowledge of what to do." She gave Angie instructions on how to hold him down while she worked with the shoulder. "It is better to do this while he is unconscious, because of the pain, you see."

Angie braced herself against Zeke, not wanting to see him suffer but understanding the need for what this woman was preparing to do.

The woman made an abrupt move, causing Zeke to jerk and cry out, then his head lolled to the side and the woman nodded, obviously satisfied. "There. Luckily the shoulder went back into place without much trouble."

Angie thought her definition of trouble might not be the same as Zeke's.

"We need to get him inside and he's much too heavy for us to carry," the woman said. She began to speak to him, rubbing his hands, while Angie watched in amazement.

When Zeke eventually opened his eyes Angie wanted to hug him in relief.

"Zeke? How are you feeling?"

He stared up at her in bewilderment. Then his gaze slowly circled the clearing until it rested on the woman who knelt beside him. She smiled, patting his hand.

"Good evening, Zeke. Do you think you can stand long enough for us to get you inside?"

He blinked. "Who are you?"

"Maria Cerventes. You and your friend found my place while seeking help. I am pleased to offer what I can, but you will need to help. Do you understand?"

He closed his eyes for a moment, then opened them and nodded. The two women helped him to sit up. He groaned, clutching his shoulder.

"Yes, it will be sore for a few days, but the worst is over, I think. We'll clean up that scalp wound once we get you inside. It may need a few stitches."

Zeke looked at Angie. "How did you find someone like her?" he asked.

She grinned. "I can't take credit, you know. She's a trained nurse. We're very fortunate to have found anyone."

Zeke managed to get to his feet, but he was still wobbly. He felt like a fool, allowing this weakness to get the best of him.

With Maria on one side and Angie on the other, he managed to walk to the cabin.

A lamp burned on a small table, lighting up one side of the long room. The fireplace gave a soft glow to the other side. The old woman pointed to a bed in the corner. "Why don't you lie down while I see about—"

Zeke interrupted. "No. I won't take your bed." He glanced around the room. It was well furnished. He pointed to a sofa near the fireplace. "I'll stretch out there for a few moments and rest."

"Whatever you wish." Maria turned away and went over to the sink where she got some water and a clean cloth. "Sit and let me check your head."

Angie felt in the way. She walked over to the fireplace and held out her hands.

Without looking around, Maria said, "I have some stew on the stove. Why don't you help yourself. There's bread on the counter. By the time you have it set out on the table, I should be through with this young man."

Zeke grinned. He hadn't been referred to as "young" in a long time. Age was definitely relative.

"Do you think you can eat?" Maria asked, cleaning his forehead and placing new bandages there.

"It certainly smells good. I guess my appetite hasn't been affected."

"Good. Once you have eaten, I have a herbal tea that will help you to rest by easing the pain you're experiencing."

Zeke and Angie sat at the small table. While they ate Zeke explained to Maria what had happened and how they hoped to find help to get out of the mountains.

Maria listened, nodding occasionally. When he finished, she said, "My son comes to check on me several times a week. I expect him tomorrow or the next day. He has a truck and could take you to a town large enough to be able to call for assistance."

Zeke nodded. "I'd appreciate that very much, if you don't mind having us stay over." He glanced around the cabin.

Maria nodded. "I can make you a bed of sorts with blankets if I can't get you to take mine."

"You've done enough, and I thank you for your generosity."

Maria got up and went over to the stove. She poured hot water into a cup, added what looked to be dry leaves, stirred it and brought it back to the table.

"Here. This should help your pain."

Zeke took a sip and made a face.

"I know. It isn't very tasteful, but it will help you to relax and rest. By morning you will be feeling much better."

By the time Angie and Maria cleared the table, washed and put the dishes away and prepared sleeping pallets on the floor, Zeke was almost asleep. "Whatever you gave me is certainly potent," he managed to say. He tugged off his boots and socks. He looked blearily around the room, then shook his head, unable to concentrate.

Maria guided him to the bed she had made for him. "Don't fight it. Just sleep," she said as he stretched out with a satisfied groan. She smiled at Angie. "He should sleep all right, but if he has any pain during the night, give him the rest of this tea."

"I can't tell you how grateful we are to have found you. Thank you so much for your first aid, your hospitality, your concern."

Maria nodded. "Most of the time I enjoy being here in the mountains near my family, but having company reminds me of how much I enjoy being around other people. This has been good for me as well." She patted Angie's shoulder. "Now, then. You must get some rest, too. We'll be able to visit more tomorrow. Perhaps my son will come. Perhaps not. But we will enjoy our visit while we can."

Maria blew out the lamp, whispered good-night and went to the other end of the cabin. She moved a heavy blanket along a rope, effectively shielding her end of the cabin from them.

Angie went over to the duffel bag. She found her pajamas and pulled them out. Glancing at Zeke, she saw that he was sound asleep. After pouring some of

the hot water into a bowl, she bathed herself before
going to sleep.

Her bed was no more than an arm's length from
Zeke. She felt strange lying there beside him. She
barely knew the man, and yet, because of the experiences they had shared, she felt as though she'd known
him for a long time.

She thought about her uncle. He must be distraught, wondering what had happened to them. She
thought about the cut oil line. What was going on here
in Mexico? Did the cut line have anything to do with
Tio's reasons for not wanting her to visit?

Why was somone like Zeke working for her uncle?
He was different, in a way she couldn't define, from
anyone who had worked for her uncle before.

Nothing seemed familiar to her anymore. The life
she had dreamed about was all part of the past and
had nothing to do with the present that she was experiencing.

She was alone with a man . . . a very attractive man,
one who made her blood sing whenever he touched
her. Tio would definitely disapprove. He had already
made his disapproval clear while they had been in
Mexico City.

What would he think of their sleeping side by side
with only an old woman sleeping behind a woolen
partition as a chaperon?

She sighed, turning on her side. There was nothing
she could do about her uncle's concern. They were
lucky to be alive. Perhaps it was their narrow escape
that made her feel so restless now, so aware of how
close she had come to dying before she had ever experienced what life and love were all about.

* * *

Hours later she awoke to the sounds of restless mutterings. She sat up and looked at Zeke. The fire had dwindled to glowing coals, still casting enough light for her to be able to see him.

She placed her hand on his chest and he immediately opened his eyes.

"Zeke?" she whispered. "Are you all right?"

He touched the bandage around his head with the tips of his fingers, then dropped his hand. He glanced around the room, then at her. "I must have been dreaming. What time is it?"

She looked at her watch. "Not quite two. Is your shoulder bothering you?"

He rubbed it and winced. "Yeah. It's definitely protesting." He shoved the blanket aside and got to his feet.

"What are you doing?"

He glanced over his shoulder as he walked away from her. "Answering nature's call," he replied, opening the door.

The air felt cold to his bare skin and he shivered. He took several deep breaths as he followed a path around to the back of the cabin. He needed to clear his head. He needed to forget the scene he'd discovered when he opened his eyes.

Seeing Angie lying so closely beside him, her hand resting on his chest, had brought his fantasies forcibly back to him.

For a brief moment he had allowed himself to forget who she was. In that moment he had enjoyed the sight of her soft beauty, her alluring body, her piquant personality. He couldn't remember the last time he had reacted so strongly to a woman.

When he returned to the cabin, Angie handed him a steaming cup.

"What's this?" Zeke took a sip and made a face. "How could I forget?" he said to himself. Whatever it was had eased his pain earlier. He needed to stay knocked out, at least until morning, so that he wouldn't be quite so aware of the woman nearby. He upended the cup, draining it, then sat down on his bed once more.

She sat beside him and they both gazed at the fire. Zeke couldn't believe how comfortable Angie appeared to be with him under those tantalizing conditions. The scene had a dreamlike quality for him, as though they had been together for years instead of a day. The rest of the world faded into nonexistence.

"Your skin looks like satin in the firelight," he murmured into the long silence that stretched between them. Tentatively he held out his hand. "I've been tempted to touch it to see if it was as soft as it looks."

She had been staring into the fire when he spoke. Now she slowly turned her head, causing her hair to slide forward over her shoulder. She said nothing when she saw his hand a few inches away from her face. Instead, she looked into his eyes and smiled.

Zeke brushed his fingertips across her cheeks. They grew pinker with his touch but she didn't move away. Her eyes glowed emerald green in the soft firelight. He traced the line of her brow, following its shape until he reached the center of her forehead. He followed the straight line of her nose before pausing at the slight indentation on her chin. Then he rubbed his thumb softly across her lips.

As though mesmerized by his sensory exploration, Zeke leaned toward her, longing to taste, as well as to touch. She tilted her face up to his, a tiny sigh escaping from her parted lips. When his mouth touched hers, he felt her lips quiver, but she didn't pull away from him.

He leaned into the kiss, wanting a chance to fully taste and explore. Shyly she pressed back, her sensitive mouth opening for him. Afraid to test his self-restraint by reaching for her, Zeke contented himself with their limited contact with each other. He turned his head slightly to improve the angle of his mouth upon hers and was startled when he felt her hands come to rest upon his chest. Every place her fingers touched him seemed to set a blaze going, shooting flames down through him, causing him to ache with the need to pull her closer so that he could feel her body pressing against him.

Stifling a moan, he brought his hands up and cupped her face as though sipping nectar from her lips. His tongue outlined and explored her mouth until he finally took possession.

She clutched him feverishly, touching his nape, her fingers burrowing through his hair, kneading his scalp like a delicate kitten.

Zeke finally lifted his head, drawing in much-needed air to his oxygen-starved lungs. Her long, thick lashes rested against her flushed cheeks as he stared down at her. The soft material of her pajama top fluttered, betraying her shallow breaths.

Slowly her lashes lifted, revealing the jewellike sparkle of her expressive eyes.

"This is definitely not a good idea, Princess," he whispered. "I've been without a woman for too long to be indulging myself in some heavy necking in front of a fireplace late at night.''

Her mouth was rosy and slightly swollen. His eyes were repeatedly drawn to its shape, invoking memories of how luscious she was, all ripe and inviting.

''You're indulging yourself?'' she repeated in a hesitant voice.

''Without a doubt. I haven't any business kissing my boss's niece, regardless of the situation in which we find ourselves.''

''What's so wrong with it?''

''We're from different worlds, Princess. No one knows that better than I.''

He found the grin she flashed at him adorable and irresistible. ''If I'm not protesting, why should you?''

He eyed her uncertainly. Although her tone was light, she couldn't disguise the unevenness of her breathing or the flush she wore so becomingly on her cheeks. Her kiss had also betrayed her lack of experience, a fact Zeke found endearing.

''I don't want to take advantage of you.'' His voice sounded rough and uneven in his ears.

''You haven't done anything I didn't want you to do,'' she pointed out shyly.

''Well, one of us needs to hang on to some sanity here.''

She nodded solemnly. ''All right. I'll let you be the sane one.'' Because her hands were still behind his back, she had no trouble pulling him closer, fitting against his chest as though she had been designed to be there. Her mouth quickly attached to his once again, this time with more bravery, as she mimicked his earlier moves.

First she allowed her tongue to outline the shape of his mouth before she nudged his lips apart and touched his tongue with hers.

Zeke wrapped his uninjured arm around her, slipping his hand beneath the hem of her pajama top. He traced each vertebra as they climbed steadily to the base of her neck. Then slowly and with infinite deliberation he circled her rib cage until his hand rested just beneath her breasts.

She could not hide her reaction to this new intimacy, but neither did she pull away from him. Initially he had meant to tease her by exposing his knowledge of her naive assumption that what they were indulging in was a harmless pastime. But when he brushed against the full-bodied warmth of her breast, he forgot about his original intent.

Her breast fit into his palm like a luscious fruit ripe for harvest. When he brushed his thumb against the crest, the tip bloomed into a hard button of temptation. Grimly Zeke fought his reaction and moved his hand to the other breast, evoking a similar response.

He had taken over the kiss, pulling her closer, setting the rhythm that he wanted to experience fully with her. She clung to him, meeting him thrust for thrust with her hot little tongue, teasing him, darting away before returning to taunt him, while her heated breasts pushed against his chest.

He eased the thin fabric from between them until she lay against his bare chest. He lightly rubbed his upper body against her aroused breasts, bringing them close enough for the tips to be stimulated by his slow, swaying movement.

Once again he reluctantly ended the kiss, but instead of apologizing, he pushed the garment aside until his lips could soothe and appease her aroused breasts.

His touch, instead of soothing, seemed to set off an exploding inferno. She whimpered, clutching him to her, and he realized . . . too late . . . what he had done.

Angie had never been aroused before. Her innocent little game had backfired on her. Zeke had known better than to continue their love play. As much as he wanted to, he had no intention of completing what they had started.

He also knew that he couldn't leave her in such a vulnerable state.

Carefully he lowered her to the blanket, shielding her with his body while he tenderly touched her where he knew the inferno was located. He cupped his hand over the nest of curls at the apex of her thighs, fervently hoping he could bring her to a satisfying conclusion to their reckless and dangerous situation.

Past restraint, she was acting on instinct alone. She lifted her hips, pressing against his hand. Gently he eased his finger into her fully aroused flesh, giving her a chance to grow accustomed to his invasion before he set a rhythm that brought her to a groaning climax within minutes.

When he felt her beginning to peak he covered her mouth with his own, effectively muffling her cry as she surged upward against him, straining . . . reaching . . . then finding the release she had been innocently searching for.

He continued to place tiny kisses on her face while he held her firmly against him.

She shook with reaction, her breath coming in soft pants until she began to get her breath once again.

Long minutes passed before she lay quietly. Eventually she raised her eyelids as though they were almost too heavy to lift and peered up at him.

"I never knew..." she began, then seemed lost for words.

"It's okay."

"But I didn't mean..." Once again she seemed at a loss.

"I know you didn't. It really is okay. Why don't you try to get some sleep now, all right?"

"But what about you? You didn't...I mean, you weren't..."

He couldn't hide his amusement while she vainly searched for words.

"It was much safer this way. You were experimenting. I didn't want the experience to destroy your faith in people, men in particular."

She stared up at him quizzically, her eyes full of questions. He sat up, turning away from her. Glancing over his shoulder, he said, "Go to sleep. I'll be back in a few minutes."

"But where are you going?"

"Just outside. Now get some sleep." He edged away from her, then stood and moved silently over to the door. Quietly he opened the door and slipped outside. His last glimpse of Angie was of her pulling the blanket over her shoulders, effectively outlining the sweet curve of her waist, hip and thigh.

He clenched his teeth to stop from groaning out loud.

Zeke knew he had done some stupid things in his lifetime, but his actions over the past hour were by far the most illogical, irrational and potentially disastrous of his career.

The pain he was experiencing in his lower body was only the beginning of what could prove to be a major catastrophe.

He never before had allowed himself to be distracted while on an assignment. It was an easy way to get himself killed.

He stood in the small clearing and stared up at the stars, praying for wisdom and for help. He would need both to successfully conclude this assignment now that he had gotten a sample of the way Angela De la Garza felt in his arms.

Five

The first thing Angie saw when she opened her eyes was Zeke asleep beside her. She raised up on her elbow and looked around.

Pale light filtered through a nearby window. She glanced at her watch and saw that it was after seven. Quietly she got up and went outside.

Sunlight peeked over the trees. It was going to be another clear day. She stretched, then followed the path around the cabin to answer nature's call.

When she returned she paused in front of the cabin, unwilling to face Zeke at the moment. Somehow she had to come to grips with her behavior the night before.

She had thrown herself at him, wanting him to hold her, to kiss her, to make love to her.

He had obliged her. Now she had to be able to look him in the eye without blushing.

She had wanted to experience life, hadn't she? She had been eager to discover what she had been missing. She had picked a man of the world who knew how to please a woman.

Now she knew.

Now she needed to forget.

She was an adult. There was no reason to let him see her embarrassment at her forwardness. In a few days she would be home with her uncle. There was nothing to be gained from having regrets. If she were honest with herself, she would admit to having no regrets whatsoever.

Zeke Daniels had taught her about her own sensuality. She had discovered a new aspect of herself. She would need to come to terms with her new knowledge.

Mentally bracing herself, she entered the cabin once again.

Zeke shifted, rolling over onto his shoulder, which immediately protested his weight. He groaned and opened his eyes. The space next to him was empty.

With a muffled oath he sat up. Where was Angie? The other end of the room lay in shadows. Maria must still be asleep. Zeke tossed his blanket aside and moved to the door. He jerked open the door and came face-to-face with Angie.

Only then did he realize how panicked he'd been by her disappearance. He allowed the door to shut behind him and leaned against the jamb.

"I didn't know what to think when I found you gone," he admitted. He rubbed his hand over his bare chest, only now remembering that he hadn't bothered to look for his shirt.

She nodded toward the path that wound behind the cabin. "I'll certainly appreciate indoor plumbing after this adventure."

He reached out and slid his hand around her nape, massaging the delicate muscles. "Did you sleep all right?" His thoughts asked a different question.

"Yes. And you?" Her eyes were filled with shadows.

He straightened, pulling her against him so that he could wrap his arms around her. After a brief pause she slipped her arms around his waist and hugged him back. They stood there in silence, absorbed with their sensory perceptions.

Finally he spoke, his voice husky. "I know I should apologize for last night. I could make excuses, blame my actions on Maria's tea, or I could be honest and admit that I've spent the last several weeks dreaming about making love to you."

She lifted her head so that she could see his face. "Weeks?" she repeated.

"From the time I first saw your picture sitting on Lorenzo's desk."

"Oh." She rested her head on his chest once more, unable to think of anything else to say.

"I don't want to complicate my life." His statement made a great deal of sense. "However, I think it's too late to avoid it."

When she looked up at him again, he lowered his head until his lips touched hers. Her newly awakened body responded with joy and she went up on tiptoe, leaning against him, her body dissolving into tingling bubbles of pleasure.

What was happening between them was a conscious choice for both of them. Sanity and safety lay in erecting a wall between them, and Zeke knew better than most the consequences of what was happening.

He should have known before he met her at the airport that her coming to visit her uncle at this time would be his downfall... personally and professionally.

A sound from within the cabin caused him to release his tight hold. He felt Angie's knees sag and quickly placed his hands around her waist. "Are you okay?" he murmured, his voice rumbling deep in his chest.

Her smile when she looked up at him was radiant. "If I'm dreaming, please don't wake me up."

"I think Maria is stirring," he said, regret in his voice.

"I'll go see if I can help her with breakfast." Angie disappeared behind the door, while Zeke followed the trail around the cabin.

During the next several hours, Angie worked beside Maria, visiting with her, while Zeke did what he could to help with any repairs he could find around her home. They waited for Maria's son, each with concern for the outcome.

Zeke didn't want to spend another night at the cabin with Angie.

Angie no longer cared if Maria's son ever appeared.

Maria hoped her guests would not be inconvenienced by an additional night in the wilderness.

When she heard the familiar rattle of her son's truck, Maria smiled delightedly. "Ah, Julio is here. I'll go explain your problem."

Zeke and Angie followed her out of the cabin at a slower pace. The man climbing from the truck embraced his mother and listened as she excitedly talked and gestured to the two of them. He glanced up at them standing on her porch and smiled while he patiently heard her story.

When he joined them on the porch, he held out his hand. "Hello. I'm Julio Cerventes. My mother has been explaining that you need a ride to town."

Zeke took the proffered hand. "Zeke Daniels . . . and this is Angela De la Garza. How far are we from town?"

Julio tilted his head in thought. "About three hours for one large enough to have phone service."

"I'd be glad to pay you for your trouble."

"I don't need payment, but if you'd like to replace the gasoline necessary to take you, I'd appreciate it."

He turned to his mother and began to question her about her health, whether she needed anything from town, and what he could do for her. She answered his questions and gave him a list for the store. Julio turned back to Zeke. "We need to get started if you want to go today."

Without a word, Angie went into the house and gathered their things, replacing them in the duffel bag. She thanked Maria for her hospitality. Zeke attempted to give Maria money, which she vehemently refused, and within minutes they were in the truck, heading down the mountainside once more.

The road Julio took was not the one they had landed on. When Zeke asked about that road, Julio explained that it connected one side of the mountain range with the other and few of the local inhabitants had reason to travel on it. Zeke realized that they would have been in dire straits if they hadn't found Maria's cabin.

Angie sat between them. In order to give Julio room to work the floor shift, she leaned against Zeke. To accommodate her, he placed his arm behind her on the seat. Before long, he noticed she had fallen asleep.

He wished he could be so relaxed around her. The scent of her floral shampoo tantalized him. He dropped his hand onto her shoulder, just to be able to touch her.

The sun was setting by the time they reached the settlement Julio had mentioned. The place was smaller than Zeke had envisioned, but Julio assured him there was telephone service to the area.

Zeke insisted on buying Julio dinner, filling his gas tank and giving him money to help with his mother's purchases. By the time they waved Julio off, night had fallen.

The only place renting rooms was a cantina on the edge of town. Zeke didn't like the idea of having Angie stay there, but there was little choice. When he asked to speak to the proprietor, the bartender pointed out an overweight man with greasy hair. Zeke took Angie's hand and walked over to the man.

"I understand you rent out rooms here?"

The man looked up from the cards he held in his hand. He glanced at Zeke then his gaze darted to Angie. The smile he gave her caused her to shiver. "Perhaps so. It would depend, of course, on how many you need and for how long." One of his front teeth was missing, which didn't dim his smile at Angie. She took a step closer to Zeke.

"My wife and I would like a room for the night. We would also like to use a phone if there's one available here."

At the word *wife* the proprietor's smile disappeared. "We have a room for you. The phone is at the front desk." He pointed to a wide doorway.

"Thanks." Zeke kept his grip on Angie's hand and escorted her into the other room, which served as the entry to the upstairs rooms.

A young man nodded. "You wish a room?"

"Yes."

"We have special two-hour rates, if you like."

"I'm sure you do. However, my *wife* and I will be staying the night. I also need to arrange transportation out of here tomorrow. Would it be possible to use your phone?"

"Certainly. We do not have phones in the room, but you may use this one."

After he paid for their room, he called Lorenzo. The phone rang only once before it was picked up.

"Yes?"

"She's okay, boss. We ran into a little difficulty and I had to put the plane down on the side of a mountain. We just reached civilization."

"Thank God! All I could think about was how much Angela had wanted to come home and how hard I tried to convince her not to come. Is she there? May I speak with her?"

Zeke handed the phone over to Angie without comment. She looked at him in surprise, then placed the phone to her ear.

"Hello, Tio? We're all right. Didn't you believe Zeke when he told you?"

"Angela! Ah, my sweet angel, I have been distraught. I have not slept since I learned your plane was missing. I am so very sorry for yelling at you. I was upset, you see. It has nothing to do with you. I love you, little angel."

"I love you, too, Tio. Zeke is taking very good care of me."

"Good, good. I'm glad he's there with you. Let me speak with him, all right?"

"We'll see you soon, Tio. Get a good night's rest, please. Hopefully we'll be home by tomorrow." She handed the phone back to Zeke.

Before he could speak, Lorenzo said, "Tell me where you are. Do you need someone to come get you?"

Zeke described their location and continued, "It would save considerable time if you could find someone to fly in and pick us up, but I'm not sure about landing strips."

"Tell me how to find you. I'll send a private helicopter. Was my Angela frightened when the plane went down?"

"She has the courage of ten men, Lorenzo. You should be proud of her."

"Oh, I am. I am."

"She's going to need all the courage she can muster to take to the air again. This hasn't been a very positive experience for her."

"Once I get her home, I'm not going to let her out of my sight!"

"I can understand that reaction."

"What about my plane. Can it be salvaged?"

"I think so, but you're going to need to send something to have it towed in. One of the wings is gone. We clipped something after we were on the ground."

"But no one was hurt?"

"No. I just bruised my shoulder a little."

"I'll have someone there to pick you up as soon after daylight tomorrow as possible. Get some rest tonight."

"I intend to. G'bye, Lorenzo."

Zeke put down the phone and turned away from the desk, a room key in his hand. With his hand at the small of her back, he silently guided Angie up the stairs.

She waited until they were inside the small room with a single bed, a wooden table and a chair before she repeated, "Your wife?"

Zeke's shoulder ached and he wasn't looking forward to the night ahead of him. "You're welcome to take your chances in a room alone, but the clientele of a place like this doesn't pay much attention to locked doors, not to mention the proprietor of the place. He was looking at you like a starving dog looks at a juicy steak."

She hugged her elbows and looked around the room.

He almost smiled. "Not much like the hotel room in Mexico City. I don't think we'd have much luck with room service, even if there *was* a phone." He walked over to the window and looked out. The room was probably the most quiet of the group. It faced away from the street. He could see a straggling line of houses listlessly climbing the hill.

When he turned back to face her, Angie sat on the edge of the small wooden chair.

"The one thing you don't have to worry about, Princess, is my taking advantage of this situation. You can have the bed and I'll—"

"No! I'm not a child. There's no reason why we can't share the bed."

"Don't kid yourself. There's an excellent reason. I don't have the energy or the willpower to leave you tonight if things get overheated... and I can't imagine sharing a bed with you and *not* having things get overheated." He walked over to the table where he had set the duffel bag. "I'm going to see if this place has a shower I can use. There's a sink over there if you'd like to wash up. I wouldn't suggest your showering tonight." He opened the door and paused, looking back. "I'm taking the key with me. Don't open the door for anyone, do you understand?"

She nodded and he closed the door.

Angie sat there hugging herself, feeling as though she were going to fly into tiny pieces if she let go of her grip. Never had it occurred to her that they wouldn't find comfortable rooms to spend the night.

Her traitorous body had already acknowledged awareness of their situation. She was aware of every move Zeke made, every breath he took, every word he said. She felt as though she would be able to find him in a crowd if she were blindfolded... by the very essence of who he was.

She had placed her life in his hands just a few days ago. It was only now that she realized she had also placed her heart in his hands, as well.

Zeke Daniels defined the word *tough*. There were no soft edges. A man like Zeke might sample something that attracted his attention, but he would never buy.

She wasn't surprised that he had worked for her uncle only a few weeks. She had a hunch he never stayed anywhere for very long.

She could never have imagined that she would give her heart to such a man because, in her innocence, she had never known such a man existed.

They would return to Monterrey tomorrow, when she would once again be the daughter of the manor and he the hired hand. He didn't seem to have any regrets about their situation. Why should he? Once he turned her over to her uncle, his duties would be finished.

Tonight would be the last night she had with him. She could literally turn her back, ignore him and fall asleep, or she could have one more night with Zeke, a night in which she would collect some unforgettable memories for the time when he would be gone.

After his shower, Zeke went downstairs to the cantina. He intended to give Angie plenty of time to get ready for bed and to fall asleep.

From the moment he realized that the only way he could protect her was to keep her in his room, he knew he was in for a sleepless night. He ordered a drink and watched a card game at the next table. When one of the men decided to leave, one of the remaining players asked Zeke if he wanted to join in. The stakes were small and from what he had observed, the game friendly. Shrugging his acceptance, he moved over to the next table and began to play.

He lost track of time because time didn't matter. All he needed to do was to get through the night. He had positioned his chair so that he could watch the stairs up to the second floor. He knew exactly who had gone upstairs and why. When the game broke up, he knew he couldn't postpone the inevitable any longer. With a nod to the other men, he headed to the room.

Quietly fitting the key into the lock, he eased the door open. The shadowy darkness of the room made it difficult for him to see anything. He closed the door and waited for his eyes to adjust before he moved.

"Zeke?" She murmured the name and he knew that she was far from awake. He smiled.

"Yes," he replied in a low, soothing voice. "Everything's fine. Get some rest."

"I waited for you...I wanted..." Her voice trailed off. She said no more. He figured her to be sound asleep, which was fine with him.

Now that his eyes were adjusting to the dark, the starlight from the window gave him enough light to see. He sat down in the chair and removed his boots and socks. Then he took off his shirt. He'd sleep in his jeans as he had done last night. Much safer that way.

He smelled of cheap liquor and cigarette smoke, although he'd only had a couple of glasses and he hadn't had a cigarette in more than five years.

Contamination by association.

He didn't want that to happen to Angie because of him. She deserved better. There was no way he could take advantage of their situation. She would hate him soon enough, when she found out why he worked for her uncle.

Her relationship to Lorenzo would be another contaminating factor, one that he couldn't protect her from, at least not entirely. However, as long as he kept his objectivity where she was concerned, he would be able to explain her innocence to those in charge and they would have no reason to doubt his word.

All of that would come later. For now, he had to get some sleep.

Zeke silently moved to the bed. With measured movements he stretched out on top of the covers, gratefully acknowledging to himself that, as tired as he was, he would have no trouble sleeping after all.

He closed his eyes and allowed the air to leave his lungs in a peaceful sigh.

Angie stirred beside him, but he continued to lie there without moving, already drifting into restful slumber. Let her think he was drunk. Let her think he was—

His eyes flew open.

Angie had pushed her covers off and was kneeling beside him, placing dainty kisses across his chest. She had neglected to wear anything to bed.

"Not fair," he groaned, his hand resting on her head. Whether he meant to push her away or hold her close, he wasn't sure.

She paused in her soft caresses and looked at him. "You took care of me last night. Now it's my turn." Her fingers found the zipper of his jeans and eased it downward, shoving his jeans and briefs down his legs until they fell off the end of the bed.

Zeke stiffened, knowing that she didn't understand, she couldn't know that—

Reverently she brushed her fingertips across his burgeoning flesh, getting an eager response from the traitorous part of his anatomy.

"Angie, noooo—"

"It's all right, Zeke. Really. I just want to—"

"I know what you want to, but it's not possible. I—"

"But you were prepared. I found this in your bag, so you must have—" She was pulling the item from its foil wrapper.

"Not you, darlin'," he breathed. "I always keep them with me. I—oh, Angie, oh honey, you don't know what that does to me. I can't— I don't have the control to—"

He lost his train of thought. Hell, he was losing his mind. For a young lady with zilch experience she was logical enough to understand design and its application for the aroused male body.

She stroked him, causing his hips to surge upward as though independent of the rest of him. "You're much larger than I thought a man would be."

He heard the quiver in her voice, but before he could think of something to say in reply, she shifted once again, this time stretching out on top of him. He could feel her full, taut breasts pressing against his chest.

The Inquisition could not have come up with a finer torture than what Angie had devised. To make matters much more difficult, she didn't have a clue of the torment in which she had innocently placed him.

"Angie, I—"

Her kiss muffled whatever he had been going to say. Openmouthed, she copied the kiss they had shared on Maria's front porch, her tongue darting to meet his in a playful duel.

Each person has his or her limit and Zeke knew when he reached his . . . then went tumbling past.

"Angie, honey," he managed to get out before she silenced him once again. He rolled so that she was lying beneath him on the bed. He ran exploring fingers along her body, feeling the taut peaks of her breasts, the quivering of her ribs from her panting breaths, and finally, when he touched her most secret place, he found that she was ready for him.

"So sweet," he whispered, knowing that he was too far gone to stop what had been put into motion tonight. He pulled one of her knees up so that her heel rested along the back of his thigh. "I don't want to hurt you," he breathed, lowering his body imperceptibly closer while he kissed and caressed her, readying her for the next step.

This time it was more than his fingers that found the barrier proclaiming her innocence. Zeke paused, squeezing his eyes shut, knowing that there was no way for him to lessen the pain she was about to feel.

"Zeke? What's wrong?" she murmured. "Am I too—"

"You . . . are perfect . . . Princess," he managed to answer between short, shallow breaths. "I don't want to hurt you, I'm so afraid—"

Once again she removed the situation from his control by hooking her heels together and lunging upward, forcing his entry. He heard her gasp and felt her quivering as she clutched him around his shoulders, holding him in a viselike grip.

When he attempted to ease away, she cried out. He held still, his weight resting on his forearms, and placed tender kisses on her upturned face.

"I didn't mean to cry out," she whispered between quick breaths. "I knew there would be some discomfort . . . I just didn't expect . . ."

"Don't apologize, Princess. Please, not that." He eased back and she sighed, lifting to him once more. He let her set the rhythm. This was her seduction. He would let her control it. . . .

Until he could wait no longer. He couldn't hold back, couldn't wait. He needed to—

Zeke took over the pace, afraid he was rushing her but no longer able to—aaahhh, there. The inner ripples were beginning to stir deep inside of her, causing her to stiffen in surprise. They continued to grow and grow, pulling him ever deeper inside until he felt swallowed up in the sensation.

He muffled her cry with his mouth, feeling his own release and knowing that he had never experienced anything remotely like this in his life. The sensations went on and on, as though they were being swept into a huge vortex forcing them deeper and deeper into the black pit of total experience ... the place without thoughts, without words, without time.

Infinity.

Six

Zeke heard a soft footfall at the top of the steps. Despite his relaxed state and the fact that he had slept deeply during the night, the tiny sound brought him into abrupt wakefulness.

Angie lay with her head on his chest in an abandoned pose that caused him an unexpected pang to see her trusting vulnerability.

He slipped out of bed without rousing her, had his pants pulled up and zipped before the soft tread paused in front of his door. Reaching into a hidden compartment of his duffel bag, he palmed his pistol and silently moved to the door.

The soft tap on the door was anticlimactic.

"Hey, Zeke. You in there? Time's awasting, man. We gotta get going."

Zeke recognized the voice of Pablo, one of Lorenzo's men. He had no more time than to release his pent up breath before he realized that the knock and voice had awakened Angie. His eyes widened with dismay as he saw her open her eyes, sit up and—

He made a dive and placed his free hand over her mouth.

"Hey, Pablo, I'm awake," he hollered. "Glad you made it. I'll go wake up Angie and see you downstairs in a few minutes."

He waited until the footsteps retreated before removing his hand from Angie's mouth. When she didn't immediately tell him off for grabbing her so unceremoniously, he turned and fully faced her. Her gaze was fastened on his other hand, her eyes wide with shock.

As casually as possible, he returned the pistol to the duffel bag and said, "We overslept this morning, Princess." He sat down and started pulling on his socks and boots. "We should have been up hours ago. Instead, we almost got caught in bed together." He stood up and stomped his feet, then reached for his shirt. "I don't like to think what Lorenzo would do to me if we'd been seen." He concentrated on the buttons. "I'm going downstairs for some coffee and, if I'm lucky, some breakfast. Give me about twenty minutes and come down as though we haven't seen each other since last night. As far as Pablo knows, I tapped on your door on the way downstairs."

When he finally looked at her, his gaze was steady.

"Why do you have a gun?"

Exasperated, he put his hands on his hips. "Did you hear a damn thing I just said?"

"Yes. I just don't understand why you have a gun."

"It's part of my job, Princess." He opened the door. "Twenty minutes, no more."

Angie was left to stare at the dingy door in silence.

Mechanically she got out of bed and walked over to the sink. There was no hot water, but it didn't matter. She found some coarse soap and scrubbed her body until it glowed.

Oh, dear God, what had she done? How could she have forgotten everything she had ever been taught? What was it in her personality that impulsively pushed all the limits, only later becoming aware of the consequences?

Why would possessing a gun be part of Zeke's job for her uncle? She didn't understand at the moment, but once she reached home she would insist on some answers.

The flight home certainly helped to get her mind off her questions. Angie hadn't known that Zeke had arranged aerial transportation to rescue them. If so, she would have insisted on something that rolled over the ground.

She hadn't been given a choice. When she had arrived downstairs, carefully following Zeke's instructions, she had met Pablo, once again alarmed at the type of individual working for her uncle. She couldn't imagine why her uncle would need a man who looked more like a wrestler or a bouncer than anything else.

Big and burly, Pablo was certainly not her idea of a pilot, but when, after breakfast, the three of them walked to the helicoptor waiting on the edge of town, Angie realized that was how Pablo had gotten there so fast.

She panicked.

"No, Zeke. Absolutely not. You can go ahead and I'll just wait here. I'll take a bus back to town...or maybe I can rent a car. I'll just— Zeke! Put me down. No! I'm not getting on— I'm not flying agai— Zeeeke!''

She had found herself unceremoniously dumped in one of the seats, her seat belt efficiently fastened around her.

Now Zeke and Pablo chatted away, pointing out areas of interest to each other as they flew much too low to the ground, while she crouched in the small seat behind Pablo.

Once in a while Zeke would look back at her. He'd give her a sympathetic smile, touch her hand or her knee as though making a silent apology.

How could he have done this to her? He knew how frightened she was of flying, particularly after what had happened to them. How could he expect her to go up in the air again when the mere thought... Something flashed from below and she looked out...and kept on looking.

After a while she forgot to be afraid. The two men were obviously unconcerned. She couldn't hear what they were saying because of the noise. She didn't care what they were saying. If they were discussing another crash, she would prefer to be taken unawares.

It wasn't that she feared death. It was the uncertainty of whether she was going to actually die or whether she was going to be subjected to unspeakable and unimaginable pain first.

But if she were to die— Ah, then she could at least appreciate her midnight behavior. Her impulsiveness had led her on a road of discovery that had swept her away into a whole new world of sensation and pleasure.

Yes, she had been foolish. Yes, she might very well live to regret her actions, but for now, all she wanted to do was to relive the night before.

She leaned her head back against the seat and closed her eyes, cleverly distancing herself from the present.

"Angie. Are you all right?"

Zeke's touch reached her at the same time she heard him calling her name.

She opened her eyes and nodded, seeing the silent question in his dark eyes.

He pointed ahead. "That's your uncle's airfield down there. You should be home soon."

She sat forward, trying to see around his broad shoulders and Pablo's bulk. The tin roof of a hangar glinted in the sun. She saw a black limousine parked nearby with a group of men watching their approach.

They looked so tiny, like little toy men with toy cars and airplanes, waiting for a child to pick them up and rearrange them to suit a young mind's fancy.

Their descent was much too fast for Angie. Her stomach seemed to stay in the air. But before she could think about her physical reaction, they were on the ground and her uncle was running toward the helicopter in a crouch, the wind from the blades blowing his suit flat against his body, his tie and hair streaming behind him.

Pablo cut the engine and the blades' whopping sound gradually lessened.

Zeke crawled out, then turned and helped Angie, lifting her by the waist to the ground. As soon as her feet touched, he stepped away and her uncle grabbed her.

"Angela! Thank God, you're safe. I never want to live through such a nightmare again. Nothing in life is worth the scare I've had." He held her for long, silent moments. She could feel the rapid beat of his heart as she lay pressed against his chest.

Eventually he let her go and looked at her. "Come. We need to get you home. You must be exhausted from your ordeal." He turned and slapped Zeke on the back. "You brought her back safely to me. For this, I owe you, my friend."

"Just doing my job, boss," Zeke replied in his low voice. He didn't look at Angie.

They were walking toward the car, Lorenzo and Angie with their arms about each other's waist, when she asked, "Who are all of those men, Tio? You look like you've recruited an army around you."

They reached the limousine and one of the men waiting at the car opened the rear door. Zeke walked around and got into the small seat facing Angie, her uncle and Pablo. Three other men jumped into the front seat.

"Ah, Angie, it's good to have you home. It's been a long time. There's been changes...some good, some not so good." Lorenzo took her hand and patted it. "We'll talk, my angel. Once you're home and settled in, we'll talk."

Angie glanced at Zeke and saw the impassive expression that he had worn so often since she first met him. Was it only a few short days ago? She felt as though she had known him forever, as though he had been a part of her life...and her dreams...since childhood. She knew that look was a shield for his thoughts and feelings. Someday perhaps he would be willing to share them with her.

"So tell me about the family, angel. What has been happening in your life since last spring?"

Obligingly Angie brought her uncle up-to-date on her life as it had existed before she met one Zeke Daniels, who in three short days had managed to turn her world upside down.

"The oil line had been severed, then spliced to come apart once we were airborne," Zeke explained later in the day as he sat across the desk from Lorenzo in his office.

"There's no chance you're mistaken, is there?"

"Nope."

"I'm glad I've sent in a salvage crew to retrieve the plane. I want the evidence."

"Who do you think they were trying to take out?"

"I doubt they cared. They knew the plane belonged to me. It was meant as a warning."

"But if we hadn't lived to tell about it, what sort of warning would that have been?"

"I would have known. I'll put in a call to the owner of the hangar. I want to find out what kind of security the man has working for him. Or it may have been one of his own employees who was willing to be bribed."

Zeke lay in the chair, utterly relaxed. "Everybody has his price, Lorenzo. You know that."

Lorenzo leaned back in his chair. "Of course. I became a success in business because I never accept no for an answer. What I have, I built for myself. I paid my way. I have made others wealthy along the way." He shook his head. "But there are those who are always too greedy. They want more and more. They see me and they want to have it all, all that I have worked for through the years. They think I'm getting to be an old man and that I'll be easy to replace."

He stared at Zeke. "They're wrong. They've already discovered this man is much stronger and smarter than they expected."

"What did you find out about the man you caught trespassing?"

Lorenzo shook his head, disgusted. "He knows nothing. He was hired to get inside the compound, to find out the layout. The man who paid him offered him an unheard-of amount of money to get in. This character felt like he'd been blessed by a miracle, money raining from the heavens, for what looked to be a simple job." The smile Lorenzo gave Zeke held no humor. "Now he better understands that there is always something expected for payment received."

"Do you know who's behind the break-in, the damage to the oil line, last month's explosion?"

"I was hoping you'd come up with some of those answers. That's one of the reasons I hired you."

"Everyone I've spoken to is too scared to talk. I'll say one thing for you, Lorenzo, you make powerful enemies."

Lorenzo nodded. "It will take someone with a great deal of power to bring me down. I don't think the man exists."

Zeke reached for the bottle that sat between them and poured a splash of the imported whiskey over the ice in his glass. When he held the bottle up to Lorenzo, the older man nodded and held out his glass.

"I can't figure you out, Daniels," Lorenzo said, after taking a sip of his drink.

"What's to figure? I'm a simple man, with simple needs."

"On the contrary. You're a very complex man...a walking puzzle. You live by a tough code. You demand a great deal from yourself. You get accused of something that you didn't do and instead of fighting, you walk away.''

"So you're still having me checked out, huh?"

"I'm trying to solve the puzzle. I don't like mysteries I can't solve. You showed up at my door at a very opportune time, just when I needed a man of your skills and talents the most.''

Zeke propped the heel of his boot on the toe of the other. "You're saying you don't believe in coincidences?''

"You're saying that's all it was?''

"No. I was out of work. There aren't too many openings for a man of—how did you put it?—my skills and talents. Rumor had it that you might be adding men to your staff.''

"How long were you out of work?''

Zeke shrugged. "A few months. I had plenty of time to think about how I wanted to handle my situation. I had several choices I could have made.'' He took a sip of his drink. "I finally decided that I didn't care that much about my reputation. I knew I had handled myself in a professional manner. In the long run, what others thought about me didn't matter. I have to live with myself. I don't have a problem with it.''

"You could have fought them...and possibly won.''

"Ah. Now there's the big tease. What, exactly would I have won? The opportunity to continue risking my neck for an organization that turned on me at the first hint of wrongdoing? I preferred to move on. I've never found that looking backward gained me much in this world.''

As Lorenzo mulled over his comments, Zeke discovered that the philosophy he'd been spouting came more from him than from the persona he had assumed for the sake of the current assignment. If the actual facts of his career were as Lorenzo had been led to believe they were, Zeke would indeed walk away from his career without a backward glance.

The revelation about himself surprised him. But upon further reflection, he discovered what he already knew to be true about himself—he offered loyalty until he discovered his loyalty was misplaced. Then it was withdrawn.

His loyalties were clear in the present instance. He wanted to put the man across from him out of business. He despised everything the man stood for. Either Lorenzo, or someone just like him, had contributed to the death of Charlie, his childhood friend.

Granted, nobody had forced Charlie to try drugs, an experiment that quickly progressed to an addiction. Charlie had changed radically and the broken man Zeke found when he came home from the air force bore little resemblance to the boy he'd grown up with. Charlie had lost his soul chasing that elusive high that would relieve him from his ever-increasing pain. Eventually he had lost his life, as well.

No. Zeke had no use for men like Lorenzo, whose greed sucked the life out of everyone around.

Now that he had gotten to know Angela, Zeke's anger had grown even colder. How could that innocent young woman have been raised by a man whose basic code of honor was so distorted by his need for power?

"So what is between you and Angela?"

If the abrupt end to the companionable silence hadn't startled Zeke, the question would have. He stared at Lorenzo, uncertain of what he had heard. "Pardon?" he asked, straightening in his chair.

"I know my niece quite well, even though I have managed to discourage her from visiting me for years. Even without knowing her well, I would imagine she is easy for most people to read. She wears her thoughts and her feelings on her face."

"I don't understand what that has to do with me."

Lorenzo took a sip from his glass, watching Zeke from over its rim. After he set the drink down, he said, "Angela has been unable to take her eyes off you since the two of you arrived."

Zeke didn't move a muscle. Nor did he drop his gaze from Lorenzo's intent stare. "I hadn't noticed."

Lorenzo shrugged. "Perhaps not. She has been discreet, at least." He sighed. "She is a very naive young woman, I'm afraid. Between her mother's family and me, we have sheltered her too much, perhaps. We have discussed with her the possibility of marrying, but she wanted to teach school for a while. I didn't have the heart to discourage her."

"Has she told you she wants to start a school in the village near here?" Zeke hoped Angie would forgive him for this reference to one of their late-night conversations.

"Is that what she told you?"

"She mentioned it, yes. She's been eager to come home to see if it would be possible, so that she could live here and teach nearby."

"I wonder why she never mentioned it to me?"

"Perhaps because she wasn't certain you would approve."

"How did you learn so much about my niece in just a few days?"

Zeke smiled. "We were involved in some rather unusual circumstances together, wouldn't you say? It's only natural that we would become more than just acquaintances."

"Angela is very impressionable."

"Do you think so? I found her intelligent with a definite mind of her own."

"You spent three nights with my niece."

Once again Zeke was still, waiting for the next salvo. Lorenzo was operating like a submarine destroyer, randomly dropping depth charges to see what he might hit. Each shot had been an attempt to startle Zeke into an admission of some kind. The fact that they hadn't worked didn't seem to discourage him.

"Yes," Zeke agreed.

"And after those three nights together, my niece can't seem to keep her eyes off you."

"Do you want to state your point, Lorenzo?"

"I want to know how you feel about Angela."

Zeke rubbed his nose with his forefinger. "How I feel? Hmm. Well. I like Angie. I enjoyed her company. I admire her in many ways."

"Did you make love to her?"

A direct hit.

Seven

___

After a prolonged silence that neither man seemed in a hurry to break, Zeke slid back down in his chair and crossed his arms.

In a casual tone that was not reflected in his intent gaze, he finally replied.

"That's none of your business." He never lost eye contact with his adversary.

Lorenzo watched him without changing expression. "I can fire you, you know. I have never tolerated insubordination from anyone."

Zeke didn't flicker an eyelash. "That's up to you."

Lorenzo leaned forward and slapped his hand on his desk. "Dammit, I want to know if you took advantage of my niece!"

"I'm not going to discuss Angela with you. If you have any questions about my behavior while I was with her, you'll have to discuss the matter with her." He uncrossed his arms and sat up. "Is there anything else? If not, I think I'm going to hit the sack. It's been a long day."

"You'll find that your clothes have been moved."

Zeke frowned. "Where are they?"

"I decided to move you into one of the upstairs bedrooms. I want you closer to the family."

"I thought you wanted me to guard you, Lorenzo. I can do that most effectively when I'm on the ground floor."

"I have others who are doing that now. I placed them there while you were gone. Now that you are back, I prefer that you sleep closer to Angela and me."

Zeke fought for control of his emotions. He would deal with all of this later when he was alone. With a sigh to denote his utter weariness, he asked, "So where am I sleeping now?"

"The second door on the right upstairs. You have a corner room that overlooks the compound. I'll be across the hall in the other corner bedroom. You should be able to hear me should I call."

Zeke stood. "I'll see you in the morning, then." He strode out of the office.

Other than when he was learning the layout of the household, Zeke had not been upstairs. He knew there were six large bedrooms, three on each side of the hallway. He would have expected Lorenzo to put Angela across the hall from him.

The question now was, which of the other four bedrooms was she in? The three bedrooms on each side of the house shared a balcony. If she was on his side of the hallway, that would give him access to her room.

Zeke knew a trap when he saw one. What he didn't understand was why.

Angie woke up early the next morning eager to greet the day. She was home! After tossing the covers aside, she went over to the French doors and opened them, letting in the pale morning light. She walked onto the balcony and peered down at the secluded walled garden below. The only access to the garden was from the formal salon, a room seldom used.

To view the scene from her balcony catapulted her into her childhood. She remembered the days she spent playing there with her imaginary friends—reading to them, playing dolls with them. She laughed from the sheer joy of being at home again and hugged herself.

The sound of a door opening and Zeke's voice caught her attention at the same time. She turned and found him in the doorway of the connected bedroom, leaning his forearm against the doorjamb. His hair was tousled, falling over his forehead. He wore a faded pair of unbuttoned jeans, his chest and feet bare.

"It figures," he muttered, dropping his forehead against his arm.

At least that was what she thought he said. But since the words made no sense, she just smiled and said, "Good morning, Zeke. Isn't it a beautiful morning?"

At her comment he slowly raised his head and, after a brief glance at the bare expanse of leg exposed beneath her short pajamas, looked east to where the sun was only now touching the sky with color.

With his attention seemingly on the sky, Zeke drawled, "You're up early, Princess."

She danced over to him, her eyes sparkling. "I know." She placed her hand lightly on his chest, enjoying the feel of his heated skin against her palm. "I didn't know this was your bedroom."

Leisurely he turned his head until he was staring down at her. "It wasn't. Your uncle moved me in yesterday."

Startled, she asked, "But why?"

"You'll have to ask him."

She studied his face but could read nothing from his expression.

"I don't understand."

"That makes two of us."

"Why would he have you sharing a balcony with me? He's always been so strict about the rules of behavior. He's lectured me over and over about the appearance of things. And now..." She tossed her head. "It makes no sense."

"Unless he's decided that it's already too late to protect you or your reputation. After all, you did spend three nights with me."

"That was no one's fault. Surely he isn't blaming you for—" She seemed to run out of words.

"I don't think *blame* is the word. He may be holding me accountable."

"Well, I shall tell him—" Her eyes widened as he suddenly clamped her hand beneath his, pinning it to his chest. "Zeke, let go of my hand. I need to get dressed and—"

"You should have thought of that sooner, Princess, before you found so much pleasure in rubbing your hand all over my chest." He continued to lean his forearm against the doorjamb while he pulled her with his other arm until she fell against him.

She chuckled, pushing away slightly so that she could see his face. "Zeke," she chided with a hint of breathlessness. "Be careful. Someone may see us."

"Let them," he muttered, hauling her securely against him with both arms and holding her. The woman was flat out driving him insane in those skimpy pajamas, her hair a tumbled mess, her eyes flashing intimate messages while her hand left paths of fire wherever she touched him.

He was a man, dammit, not a machine. He wasn't immune to her charms. On the contrary, their night together had made him ache for her, increasing his desire rather than appeasing it.

As soon as his mouth covered hers, she melted against him like molten lava, her curves fitting to his, her arms snaking around his waist.

This was the reason he hadn't been able to sleep well the night before. He'd known she was sleeping somewhere nearby. He could almost sense her presence. He couldn't seem to get enough of her, even now when he held her snug against him.

With a muffled oath, he swooped her up and hauled her into his room, nudging the door to the balcony closed behind them with his foot. They were in bed in a few quick strides.

Angie was as aroused as he. With trembling fingers she jerked her pajama top over her head, then stuck her thumbs into the waistband of the shorts and slid them off, leaving her bare as she knelt before him. Zeke unzipped his jeans, peeling them off without taking his eyes from her.

When they reached out to each other there was almost an audible sound of combustion. Their hands and mouths were touching and tasting, stroking and caressing, feverishly grasping each other. They fell back onto the bed in a tangle of limbs, seeking relief from this hot desire that had exploded between them.

Whimpering from need, Angie pulled him to her. He lifted her hips and lowered his head, kissing her until she cried out. Then in one surge of male domination he claimed her, filling her while at the same time he covered her mouth with his own.

He kept the pace at fever pitch—never slackening—even when he felt her arch beneath him. Her trembling increased into convulsive spasms that began to squeeze him in a relentless rhythm he couldn't resist. He lost control, filling her with his seed.

His unprotected seed.

The lack of protection only occurred to Zeke long minutes later when he was sprawled out beside her, too limp to move. He'd been too inflamed with his need for her...in his frenzy to claim her he had forgotten to consider any consequences.

He'd totally lost his mind. There was no doubt about that any longer. He was now certifiably insane. How could he have—

She stirred, leaning over him, kissing his nipples with a feathery touch.

He groaned.

Whatever she thought she could stir up at this stage, she was wrong. There was no way his satiated body could respond. He had exhausted himself...totally and completely.

Her kisses trailed downward until she touched him intimately.

Maybe not completely.

How could he be responding, when his arms, his legs—hell! the entire rest of his anatomy!—seemed to have the muscle power of overcooked spaghetti?

He gave up wondering and closed his eyes, drowning in the pleasurable sensations she evoked.

After she performed a miracle that had Zeke gasping, she moved over his inert body, placing her knees at either side of his waist, and lowered herself until she surrounded and enfolded him in her fiery warmth.

Her movements were delicate and gentle all the while she brushed light kisses across his face and neck. With an enticingly deliberate movement, she came up on her knees, then slowly lowered herself, setting a rocking rhythm that was rapidly building tension throughout his body.

He opened his eyes and stared up at her. She wore a dreamy expression that touched his heart. "Oh, Princess, I'm not believing this," he whispered.

"Just relax and let me love you," she whispered back.

He would have laughed if he'd had the strength. "Relaxing is beyond my capabilities at the moment. What you're doing to me should be outlawed, it feels so good."

"I want to give you pleasure," she murmured. "You have taught me so much. I can never repay you."

He grasped her waist, pulling her down so that her breasts were there in front of his face. He began to tease her with his tongue and mouth, touching and tugging until her breathing became ragged.

Zeke took over the rhythm, guiding her faster against him until she gasped out her release at the same time he felt his. This time she collapsed against him and lay on top of him, unmoving.

He didn't have the energy or the strength to move her.

They fell asleep in that position.

"Good morning, Tio," Angie sang as she came into the breakfast room where Lorenzo and Zeke were eating. She leaned over and kissed her uncle on the cheek. "Isn't this the most beautiful morning?" She pulled out one of the chairs and sat before either man could assist her. "Good morning, Zeke. Did you sleep well?"

Zeke had known he was in big trouble as soon as she came through the door. She glowed, radiating contentment and goodwill, looking adorable. How had this slip of a woman managed to wrap him so securely around her little finger?

And did she have to look quite so well loved this morning? A blind man would have noticed the sheen of sexual satisfaction on her face, and Lorenzo was far from blind.

He met her gaze with an impassive one of his own. "I slept passably well, under the circumstances. And you?"

"What circumstances?" Lorenzo growled, looking up from his meal.

Zeke arched a brow. "Another new bed to adjust to. I haven't slept in the same bed twice in several days."

"Oh." Lorenzo looked back at his breakfast.

Angie caught Zeke's eye and grinned, obviously delighted with herself. He held her gaze without smiling and said, "Lorenzo, I'd like to have a few moments of your time after breakfast, if possible."

The older man nodded without comment.

"I thought I'd go to the village this morning, Tio, if you have no objections. I want to look around, visit with some of the young mothers, talk with them about the possibility of starting a preschool."

Lorenzo carefully replaced his eating utensils beside his plate. "Does that mean you don't intend to return to Madrid?"

Her clear-eyed gaze met his. "Don't you want me here?"

The gauntlet lay on the table. Zeke took a sip from his cup and waited.

"It isn't a case of not wanting you. I'm concerned for your safety. Zeke said you knew the problem with the plane was not an accident. The plane wasn't the first problem with sabotage I've run into. You asked yesterday why I have so many men working for me? Well, I needed to increase the security around here in order to ensure everyone's safety."

Angie had been filling her plate while he talked. When he paused, she looked up and said, "Why are these things happening?"

"Because of my success. Someone is trying to take over. I've had problems at the farms who sell me their wool, the manufacturing plant continues to have delays and inexplicable breakdowns. Several of my shipments into the States have been stopped at the border."

"You think a competitor is doing this?"

"Or someone who is determined to drive me out of business in any way he can."

She glanced at Zeke before looking back at her uncle. "Is that why Zeke works for you?"

"Yes. He's been immensely helpful in setting up some defense strategies."

"I see." She studied her plate thoughtfully, then picked up her fork and began to eat.

After a brief silence, Lorenzo said, "If you still want to go to the village, I'll send one of the men with you. Anyone who knows me knows that you are very dear to me. I don't want to take a chance on someone trying to harm you."

She reached for Lorenzo's hand and squeezed it. "Thank you for explaining, Tio. I love you. I don't wish to make anything more difficult for you. This is why you didn't want me to come home, isn't it?"

He nodded. "I had hoped to resolve some of these problems before you came." He smiled at her. "I must admit, however, that I'm very pleased you're here. I have no desire to see you leave, ever again."

Zeke shoved back his chair. "I have a few things I want to check on. I'll meet you in your office in half an hour, if that's all right."

"Fine."

Zeke had to get out of there before he said something. How could a man who obviously loved his niece put her through all of this? Why didn't he just turn himself in and let the authorities handle it? Why would he want to jeopardize her life?

He had been mulling over what he was going to do about the situation since he woke up the second time that morning. Angie had still been asleep, a soft smile shaping her mouth. He'd thought about it during his shower, getting dressed, and during his silent breakfast with Lorenzo.

He had to use his own judgment. He had to decide what he could do that would benefit everyone and still have the desired outcome.

Somehow he had to devise a plan that would protect Angie from what was going to happen to her uncle.

When Zeke walked into Lorenzo's office, the older man nodded. Zeke sat down across the desk from him.

"What's on your mind?" Lorenzo asked.

"I want to know what your game is."

Lorenzo raised his brows. "I'm not following you."

"Why did you choose to put me in the bedroom next to Angie's?"

Lorenzo almost smiled. "How do you know I did?"

"I know. So why are you setting me up?"

Lorenzo picked up a pen on his desk and began to turn it end over end. After a long silence, he said, "I've noticed the interest you've taken in my niece from the beginning. You were fascinated by her picture from the day you first walked into my office."

"Your niece is a beautiful woman. How could I not notice?"

"You need to understand that Angela is the only family I have left. I loved and admired her father. He was my hero. When I lost him and his wife, I vowed to make up their loss to Angela. I never wanted her to go without anything. I've worked years to ensure that she would be financially secure."

Dropping the pen onto the desk, he looked at Zeke. "What I finally came to realize is that Angela needs a strong man who can look after her interests once I'm gone."

Zeke began to see where this conversation was headed. He felt cold beads of moisture form across his forehead. He was right. He'd been set up.

"I want you to know that I don't intend to stand in the way of a relationship between you and Angela."

"A relationship," Zeke carefuly repeated.

Lorenzo nodded. "Yes. My Angela is a woman now. I have seen the way she looks at you, the way she behaves around you. I know you're attracted to her, as well."

Zeke continued to stare at him without expression, his mind racing with all the implications of Lorenzo's words.

"You want me to marry your niece," he finally stated in a neutral tone.

Lorenzo smiled. "Would that be so bad?"

"You know nothing about me, Lorenzo. Neither does she."

Lorenzo nodded. "Which is exactly why I re-checked your background. You've had an interesting life. You're a tough man, but from everything I've been able to determine, you've been a fair one. You would care for Angela, I believe, and protect her from harm."

"You don't question me about loving her."

Lorenzo shrugged. "Whether you love her at this point or not, you want her. I've seen it in your eyes. You're what she needs. She is what you want. I have reason to think the alliance would work."

"What about her feelings regarding all of this?"

"I'll leave all of that to your discretion. It's up to you to court her. I'm telling you that you will run into no obstacles where I'm concerned."

"On the contrary, you've decided to keep us in close proximity."

"And let nature takes its course . . . yes."

"What makes you think I want marriage from her?"

"I don't. However, rest assured I'll slit your throat if you dishonor her. You have my promise on that."

Zeke studied the older man for a moment. "You missed your calling, boss. You should have been a matchmaker."

"Don't hurt her, Zeke."

"She knows nothing about me, about my background. She would be appalled to know what I've done in the past."

"She doesn't ever need to know. You have a new profession here, taking over my position someday. Men are plotting to take what I am freely offering you."

Zeke stood. "You're placing a great deal of trust in me, Lorenzo."

The older man stood, as well. "Yes."

Zeke was the first to turn away.

Zeke left the house and remained gone all day. He talked with the men who were on guard duty at the gate of the compound. He checked with the men in charge of the guard dogs and the surveillance cameras.

He avoided both Lorenzo and Angie, because he needed time to think. By the time he returned to the house that night, only the men on guard in the house were stirring. Silently Zeke climbed the stairs and entered his room.

After a long, hot shower he pulled on his jeans and stepped out onto the balcony, breathing in the tranquillity of the night air. There were no sounds in the house or the courtyard. The walled garden looked serene in the starlight. He noted that Angie's doors were closed but made no effort to discover if they were locked.

As much as he had missed her today, as much as he wanted to see her now, he knew that if he saw her, he'd ignore all the reasons why he had to leave her alone and he'd make love to her.

How could this situation have happened to him? Never before in his career had he allowed himself to become emotionally involved . . . either with the situation or with a person.

However, he had to face the fact that he was deeply involved in this situation and there was no one with whom he could discuss the matter. Frank had been adamant about not breaking his cover for any reason.

He muttered an unprintable word under his breath.

The irony of the situation didn't escape him. Lorenzo was actually grooming him to take his place! If the plane incident hadn't been so dangerous, he might suspect Lorenzo of having planned for them to be marooned together. Had Lorenzo's anger that first night been an act? Had he hoped that Zeke would stay with Angie, anyway, taking advantage of the situation?

The ensuing nights had certainly played right into Lorenzo's hands to further his own personal agenda. What if Lorenzo *knew* Zeke was working for the United States government? What if he were using Angie as the Judas goat to lure Zeke into the trap? If so, the trap should be ready to be sprung at any time.

Was Angie aware of how she was being used, as well? He thought back over the past few days and knew beyond any doubt that she was as innocent as she appeared, which made what Lorenzo was doing even more reprehensible. Lorenzo was in such a habit of manipulating the people and events around him that he didn't hesitate to sacrifice the only family member he had.

Zeke knew that he had to do something, and soon. He was going to have to risk discovery and get into that office, perhaps bluffing his way out if he were caught.

He couldn't afford to hang around here much longer if he expected to get out alive.

The only question remaining now was Angie. Could he walk away, leaving her to face all the consequences alone? How was she going to be able to cope with knowledge of who and what her uncle really was? Everything she had ever believed in, had ever loved, would be turned upside down, if Zeke was successful.

He felt a strong surge of pain rush through him. He gripped the railing of the balcony and closed his eyes. How could he knowingly cause her such anguish?

However, he'd made a commitment, he'd agreed to this assignment, and a great many lives depended on his carrying out his duties. There had been times in his life when he didn't much like himself or the career he had chosen.

Tonight was one of them.

He had destroyed her innocence. He had also risked getting her pregnant. Was he going to walk away and let her deal with the possible consequences alone?

He'd always been willing to pay for every decision he made. Could he turn his back on her now, know-

ing the price would be more than she could face alone?
If she was pregnant and he left her, the disgrace would
destroy her.

But he sure as hell didn't intend to hang around here
and take over Lorenzo's flourishing drug trade!

Zeke wrestled with his demons for several hours
until he decided on the only course of action he could
live with.

Eight

Angie snuggled against Zeke's large, warm body, loving the sensation of being pressed against the muscled surface, enjoying the feel of his warm breath against her cheek—

Her eyes flew open! Zeke was indeed in bed with her. This was no dream. He lay stretched out beside her, propped up on one elbow, watching her.

"Zeke! What are you doing in here? I—"

"What does it look like I'm doing?" he murmured, leaning down and nuzzling beneath her ear.

"I mean, how did you get in here? I remember locking the door."

"Which wasn't very neighborly of you, was it?" He dipped his head and kissed the hollow between her breasts, revealed through her sheer cotton top.

"I didn't want the maid to come in and find you here in the morning."

He straightened, frowning. "Is there a possibility of that?"

"Yes. I wasn't in my room when she came in this morning. I had to make up a tale about where I was." She met his gaze. Her voice wavered slightly as she said, "We almost got caught."

"It certainly sounds that way, doesn't it?" he replied in a mild voice.

She eyed him uncertainly. "Don't you even care?"

"Actually, I do. That's why I'm here. I thought we needed to talk about the matter privately, without interruption." He didn't mention that he'd almost forgotten why he'd picked her lock and entered her room once he saw her lying there on the bed. She slept like a child, bonelessly relaxed, sprawled across the bed.

She touched his cheek. "I know I've been very foolish, allowing my attraction to you to lead me to behave in a way I never would have believed possible." She sighed. "Tio would be devastated if he knew." She dropped her gaze. "I had no idea I could be so weak."

"The thing is, Princess," he began slowly, as though picking his words with care. "There's a good chance that you may be pregnant."

Angie froze. His words had caught her completely off guard. She thought back over the intimate moments they had shared, her eyes widening with realization. "You mean when we—"

"Yes. When I didn't protect you."

She bit her lip, shaken by the fact that she had never considered the possibility. "I never thought about it. I just—"

"Yeah, well, I've thought about it. It's been on my mind all day. I've been trying to work out what to do and I think I've come up with a plan." Once again he paused.

"Well, we can wait to see—"

"Do you honestly think I'm going to be able to keep my hands off you for the next few weeks, Princess? You're damned addictive and I'm permanently hooked. I need a lifetime with you."

She stared at him, uncertain of what he was trying to say. "I don't think I understand, Zeke."

"I want you to marry me."

Her mind blanked out with shock. When she could think again, she managed to say, "You would marry me, even though we've only known each other a few days? I thought I was the impulsive one, but even I wouldn't consider—"

"You do realize, don't you, that your uncle will horsewhip me if he discovers I've been in your bed? Surely you want to spare me that fate." Although the corners of his mouth were slightly curled into a half smile, Zeke's gaze had never been so intent.

She stared at him, bewildered. "You're really serious, aren't you?"

"Yes."

"Do you really want to marry me? I mean, this isn't just a polite gesture on your part?"

The smile he gave her melted her heart. "I want to marry you and to keep you safe more than anything in the world."

Was it possible she was still dreaming? Any moment now she would wake up and discover that she was alone, that Zeke hadn't come into her bedroom, that he hadn't—

"I don't think Tio will approve. We've only known each other a few days. He will insist—"

"Do you trust me, Princess?"

She couldn't resist smoothing her fingers across his cheek. "With my life."

He closed his eyes briefly as though her words caused him pain. Then he said, "I want us to elope...now...tonight. We'll come back in a few days, after he's had time to adjust to the idea. By then our marriage will be an accomplished fact and he'll recognize that there's nothing he can do but accept the matter."

"Tonight! But, it's—" She glanced around the room. "Are you sure we should do this?"

"Absolutely."

She rubbed her forehead, distracted. "My uncle will be furious with me. It will bring back memories of my younger school days when I was always doing something to shock the nuns."

He kissed her before saying, "Honey, I'm guessing the nuns would be pretty shocked with your behavior with me already. Getting married is the best damage control there is at this point."

"But we can't just leave. Tio will wonder what happened, where we are. He'll be worried and upset."

"I thought of that. I've decided to leave him a message in his office. That way we know that he'll be the only one to find it."

"But he keeps his office locked."

"I'm aware of that. I'm also aware there are guards downstairs. However, I'm willing to take the chance if you are. I also know a way to get out of the compound without causing a stir. It's much easier to get out of here than it is to get inside. So why don't you gather a few things while I go downstairs? If I'm not back in half an hour, the safest thing for you to do is to go back to bed and forget we ever had this conversation.''

"The safest thing? You aren't making sense. Leaving my uncle a note isn't dangerous, Zeke.''

Once again he kissed her. "It is when I'm attempting to steal his most prized possession. I'll be back as soon as I can."

Zeke left her room through the balcony doors, leaving Angie bemused by the sudden turn of events.

Zeke didn't like the odds against him tonight but knew he was out of time. He had to get into Lorenzo's office without being discovered and he had to get Angie to a place of safety.

He didn't want to think about Frank's reaction when he told him that he'd married Lorenzo De la Garza's niece. More than likely he would be looking for a new job, and the current story going around about him would be validated.

Zeke left his room by way of the balcony. He lowered himself over the side and allowed himself to drop to the ground, landing in a crouch. The salon was next-door to Lorenzo's office. He could stay in the salon until the hallway was clear, then hope his skills picking the lock were sufficient to get him inside in the least amount of time possible.

He eased open the outside door to the salon, thankful that no one had thought to check it after he had unlocked it earlier in the evening. Once inside, he slipped through the shadows and cracked open the hallway door.

Two of the men stood by the stairway talking. He waited with trained patience until the conversation had been completed. One of the men headed toward the front of the house, the other toward the back, leaving the hallway empty.

Zeke reached into his pocket for the slivers of metal he needed and eased the door open. He moved without sound to the office and worked the lock, relieved to hear it quietly click in less than a half minute.

He stepped inside, closed and locked the door, and waited for his eyes to adjust before edging toward the desk. He knew Lorenzo kept his records on a personal computer and gave silent thanks he had a working knowledge of the machine.

Using only the light from the screen, Zeke wasted precious moments in an attempt to find the access code. With sudden inspiration he tapped in the name ANGELA and was offered the directory.

There was too much for him to scan. The safest course was to copy as much as possible, choosing the files that looked to be the most promising.

He found the drawer where Lorenzo kept floppy disks and went to work. Every muscle was tense as he listened for any sound from the hallway. So far, everything was quiet.

As soon as he could, Zeke finished copying the files and pocketed the disks. He would leave Lorenzo a note as he promised Angie he would. Leaving the computer screen on for light, he took a sheet of stationery and wrote,

Lorenzo,
I decided to follow your advice and marry Angela. Know that I will always take care of her.

                                        Z

Now all he had to do was to get out of there without being spotted.

Several hours later Zeke glanced over at Angie, asleep in the seat beside him in his car. She had slept through most of the night, which was just as well. They would soon be reaching Reynosa, where he intended to stop to get married.

As he guessed, they had had no difficulty leaving the compound. He had hidden her in the back seat once they reached the garage where he kept his car. When he stopped at the gate, he told the men on duty that he was restless and planned to drive into Monterrey to look for a little action. They had laughed at his words and waved him on. Once they were out of sight of the gate, he had pulled over and had Angie join him in the front seat.

He knew she understood that the men would not have been so quick to wave him through if they had known she was with him.

When she asked him where they were going, he explained that he intended to drive to Reynosa. By the time they reached the border city, the government offices should be open and they could get a license. He had taken her hand and laid it on his thigh, where it still rested. Her trust and acceptance had only added to his guilt, but he knew he could live with his guilt easier than he could walk off and leave her to what was coming once he got the information he had to Washington.

"Angie, we're almost there," he said quietly.

She stirred and opened her eyes. In a drowsy voice she said, "I was dreaming about Tio. He's going to be upset that I didn't give him a chance to be at my wedding. He was pleading with me in my dream.''

Zeke reached for her hand. "I still think this is the best way, Princess. Wouldn't you rather him be a little hurt because we ran off to marry, rather than have to face him with the news that you're not married...and pregnant?''

She pressed her hand to her middle and sighed. "I don't wish to hurt him at all. I wonder how many times I have thought that, and said it, after I did something without thinking it through.'' After a moment, she said, "Tio will also be very angry with you, you know. What if he fires you? What will we do?''

He smiled. "I think I'll be able to find a way to support you." He squeezed her hand. "Or maybe I'll put you to work to support me.''

"You're teasing me, but I could, you know.''

He raised her hand to his lips and kissed her knuckles. "I have a hunch you could do anything you set your mind to do.''

She glanced up at him. "I'll take that as a compliment, even though you may not have meant it that way.''

Zeke laughed and replaced her hand on his thigh. He liked feeling her touching him.

He turned onto a main thoroughfare. He used to spend considerable time here in Reynosa with Charlie when they were teenagers. He would find the office issuing licenses and find a judge to marry them. He wanted the marriage legal in case Frank or someone else in the bureaucracy attempted to ignore his attempt to bind Angie to him before all hell broke loose.

Later that morning they crossed the Texas-Mexico border. Zeke explained to the official at the border

that they had just married and showed him the certif-
icate. He pointed out that he was a United States citi-
zen and that Angie would get her papers updated as
soon as possible.

Once he was officially across the border into Texas,
Zeke felt the tension leave him. The first big hurdle
was past. He glanced over at Angie.

"Are you hungry?"

"A little."

He found a restaurant near the airport in McAllen
and pulled into the parking lot. As soon as they ordered, he excused himself and headed for the phones.
By the time he returned, their order was on the table.
He saw the questions in her eyes when he slid into the
bench seat across from her, but for the moment ignored them.

"This looks great. I didn't realize how hungry I
was." He quickly demolished the food on his plate in
silence, finished his coffee and asked, "Are you ready
to go?"

She smiled. "Go where?"

"That's a surprise. I've been arranging our honeymoon."

Her eyes widened. "Really?"

"But the only way we can get there is to fly."

"Oh, Zeke!" she wailed.

"I know. But the plane will be large and I'll be right
there beside you."

She shook her head. "Couldn't we go someplace
closer, so that we could drive?"

"I have to deliver something important before I can
be free to enjoy some time with you." He took her
hand. "You'll be all right. I promise."

She sighed. "Something tells me I don't have a choice."

He slid out of the bench seat and extended his hand to her. After a moment she took his hand and followed him from the restaurant. "Just because we're married doesn't mean that I'm always going to let you tell me what to do, you know."

He waited to respond to her provocative remark until he got into the car. "I wouldn't dream of always telling you what to do, Princess. Why, I'll treat your every wish as my command from now on."

She watched his profile as he pulled into traffic and followed the street signs to the airport. "My *every* wish?" she asked, intrigued by the idea.

"Weelll," he drawled, "maybe we could negotiate on a few of them."

"I thought so! You're already trying to weasel out of your promise."

He hugged her to him, but waited until he'd found a place in the long-term parking lot and stopped the car before he grabbed her and gave her a leisurely... and very thorough... kiss. They were both flushed when he finally released her.

"Enough of that, woman! You're damned distracting, did you know that?"

They claimed their tickets and found the right gate for the plane that was leaving for Dallas, where they would catch a connecting flight into Washington, D.C. He'd called Frank and told him to meet him at the airport without telling him that he would not be alone.

The main thing was that he had gotten the necessary information without blowing his cover, and had gotten himself out of Mexico safely. He'd successfully completed his assignment and as far as he was concerned, he was on his own time once he turned over the disks to Frank.

If Frank was upset, let him fire him. He'd discovered by working with Lorenzo that he had some decidedly marketable skills in the security business. He could always hire himself out as a consultant.

The main thing he had to do was to be there for Angie when she discovered the truth about her uncle.

Zeke spotted Frank in the crowd of people waiting for the passengers to disembark. He wore a pullover shirt and casual slacks, blending in with the people around him. Zeke gave a slight nod when they made eye contact, and waited for the slower passengers ahead of them to get out of his way.

By the time he and Angie were clear he had taken her hand. He stopped in front of his boss, who wore an unprofessionally startled look.

"Hi, Frank! It was great of you to agree to meet us and give us a ride to my place. I told you I had a surprise for you—" Which was a lie. He hadn't told Frank anything but the time of his arrival, when he'd asked him to meet him at the airport. "Here she is. Angie De la Garza and I were married this morning." Before Frank could respond, Zeke continued. "Angie, I want you to meet an old air force buddy of mine, Frank Carpenter. We go back several years together, don't we?"

Frank had his emotions under control, and the smile he gave them both was affable and admiring. "One thing I have to say about you, Zeke, you're a fast worker. I didn't even know you were seeing anyone." He turned to Angie and held out his hand. "I'm pleased to meet you, Mrs. Daniels. I can see that Zeke deserves congratulations.''

Angie's cheeks were pink and her smile radiant. ''I'm very pleased to meet you, Mr. Carpenter,'' she said in her fluent English. ''I must admit that Zeke keeps surprising me. I had no idea where we were going when we left Texas.''

Zeke slipped his arm around her waist and hugged her to him. ''I won't let anything happen to you, believe me.'' He kissed her on the tip of her nose, then looked up at Frank, knowing that his boss also got the message.

''The car's this way,'' was Frank's only comment, as he started down the concourse.

The men rode in the front seat while Angie took in the sights from the back seat of Frank's car. Zeke reached over and turned on the radio, setting the sound to come from the back speakers, which he knew would effectively muffle the conversation in the front seat.

''That too loud?'' he asked, glancing over his shoulder. Angie smiled and shook her head, returning her gaze to the sights and sounds beyond the window.

In a barely perceptible tone, Frank muttered, ''Are you out of your mind? De la Garza! Who is she, his daughter?''

''Niece,'' Zeke replied, without looking at Frank.

''Did you abort the assignment?''

''You know me better than that. The information you need is on the disks in the newspaper I just laid at my feet. I'll leave it there when we get out of the car.''

''What in the hell do you think you're doing marrying a member of the family?''

"She doesn't have anything to do with it. She has no idea what's been going on."

"Does she know who you are?"

"Yes. Just not what I do."

"Dangerous way to begin a marriage, wouldn't you say?"

"My choices were limited. I did the best I could under the circumstances to protect her."

"So it isn't a real marriage, then. You're removing her from the scene?"

Zeke was silent. His first reaction had been to deny Frank's statement before he remembered that he hadn't given a thought to anything other than getting her away from a potentially explosive situation. Wearily he ran his hand over his face. "Something like that, I guess."

"How do you think she's going to take it when she finds out the truth?"

"I'll deal with that when the time comes. In the meantime, I'm requesting some time off."

Frank's mouth curved slightly. "For a honeymoon?"

Zeke cut his eyes around. "Maybe."

"Can't say I blame you." He glanced into the rearview mirror. "However, you may have a tiger by the tail once she finds out the truth."

"Believe me, I've thought about that. I'll just have to deal with her reaction when it comes."

"Are you going to tell her the truth?"

"Not until he's arrested. I don't want to take the chance she'll warn him."

"She may never forgive you."

"That's the risk I'll have to take."

Frank smiled. "I'm still in shock. I never pictured you as a knight rushing to a fair maiden's rescue before. That's quite an image adjustment, let me tell you."

Zeke turned his head and looked at his superior without expression. "Go to hell," he muttered, before he too watched the traffic and the scenery.

Zeke fished his keys out of his pocket as they walked down the hallway to the apartment he'd rented the year before when he'd been recalled from his European post. "You'll have to excuse the place. I haven't been here in months. I just hope it's livable."

Angie felt as though she'd received one shock after another since Zeke had awakened her from a sound sleep last night. She wasn't certain how many more she could handle in one day. "Why haven't you ever mentioned to me that you had an apartment in Washington?"

He shrugged. "I guess I never considered the information important enough to bring up. I had to live somewhere once I left my European job. I haven't used it very much, but since I hate staying in hotels, it was worth keeping for whenever I was in town."

He opened the door and motioned for her to go inside. Instead, she asked, "Don't you intend to continue working for Tio?"

Zeke placed his hand at the small of her back and guided her into the musty-smelling apartment. He closed the door and edged her over until the door was at her back. He leaned into her, resting his forearms on either side of her head.

Nuzzling her ear, he whispered, "We've got the rest of our lives to get to know everything about each other, sweetheart. At the moment, I'm kinda distracted." He raised his head enough to find her lips with his. He continued to kiss her while he allowed his aroused body to settle firmly against her, more fully explaining his distraction.

Angie went up on her toes and wrapped her arms around his neck. She forgot all of her questions and all of her confusion. She even forgot her guilt about running away with Zeke. She couldn't deny her love for this man and would have followed him willingly wherever he suggested.

He scooped her up in his arms and headed down the hallway. "I'll show you around later," he growled, giving her short, hard kisses until he reached the side of a large bed. "For the moment I intend to keep you right here."

Zeke grabbed the bedspread with one hand and jerked it off the bed before he lowered her to the surface. She had become an addiction with him. No matter how many times he made love to her, he could never seem to get enough of her.

He refused to think about the future. Not at this moment, anyway.

He needed this woman now.

His woman.

His wife.

Nine

"Oh, Tio, Zeke has been showing me around Washington," Angie said into the phone. "He's been a wonderful tour guide since we arrived."

Zeke grimaced at Angie's praise of his abilities, remembering his earlier thoughts on the subject of becoming a professional tour guide. He sat across the room from Angie, watching her speak to her uncle on the phone. He knew that Lorenzo would insist on talking to him in a few minutes and was mentally preparing himself for the verbal assault.

He'd managed to delay the inevitable phone call to her uncle for three days now, but had recognized that morning that he could no longer postpone contacting Lorenzo De la Garza.

He'd been waiting for some word from Frank, hoping that the information he'd gotten to him would be acted upon immediately. But time had run out and

Angie had begun to fret about her uncle, afraid he'd be worried about her, despite the message Zeke had left for him.

"I don't know, Tio," she was saying into the phone. She looked over at Zeke and grinned. "Zeke hasn't said. Here, I'll let you speak with him." Angie handed the cordless phone to Zeke, whispering, "He wants to know when we're coming home."

Zeke took the phone. "Hello, Lorenzo," he drawled, and waited for the explosion.

"Once I got over the initial shock, I realized what you had done, Zeke," Lorenzo said gruffly.

Zeke froze, then murmured, "What do you mean?"

"You wanted to get Angie as far away from what's going on around here as possible. You also knew her reputation would be damaged if she continued to travel alone with you. I understand that. I just wish you hadn't spirited her away in the middle of the night. So although I can appreciate your motives, I resent the manner in which you've carried them out."

"Well, I, uh—"

"In addition, I didn't appreciate the manner you chose to show me the vulnerability of my office security. How did you manage to get inside?"

"It wasn't that difficult, Lorenzo."

"None of the men saw you anywhere near the office. The video cameras didn't pick up anything, either. The only ones who reported seeing you at all were at the gate and they swore you left alone. Were you trying to make me look like some kind of fool, Zeke?"

"Of course not. I—"

Lorenzo gave a loud sigh. "You're good at what you do, Zeke. Damn good. I should be relieved to have you on my side, but it concerns me that someone—

anyone—was able to breach the security of my office. What if you had been one of my enemies?''

Zeke met Angie's anxious gaze, then looked away. Once again guilt gnawed at him. He had no one else to blame for his present predicament. He also knew that if he had to relive the past few days, he would make the same decisions.

But the gnawing at his conscience didn't go away.

"I wanted to let you know that Angie is safe, Lorenzo. She's wanted to call, to explain—''

"I know. She told me. I won't pretend that I'm pleased at the way you went about things. I would have wanted to be there, to give her away, to take part in the ceremony." Once again Lorenzo sighed. "But it's done, now, and there's no point in continuing to belabor the point. Once we get this mess cleared up and it's safe to have visitors again, I'll have a celebration dinner and dance, introduce you to all of our friends and family." Lorenzo's voice lightened. "At least I've got some good news regarding the attempted break-ins.''

"Let's hear it.''

"I finally got a name—Benito Perez. I'm currently having him investigated, but I think we've identified our man.''

"Have you ever heard of him before?''

"Yes. He wanted to buy into one of my companies…become a partner with me. I told him I worked alone. He wasn't pleased but I haven't heard anything further from him.''

"What about the plane? Did you hear who was behind the cut oil line?''

"I spoke to the owner of the company who owns the hangar. I've used their facilities for years. He was shocked to hear about the accident and is currently having all personnel interrogated. It's possible we can trace something back to Perez." He paused, then reluctantly said, "I'll admit to sleeping better nights knowing that Angela's safe with you. I suppose you did what you felt best. I'm paying you for your judgment calls. I don't suppose I'll always agree with them, especially where my niece is concerned. She sounds happy enough, and I've only got myself to blame in the first place for suggesting you consider marrying her." In a brisk change of voice, he added, "Give me a number where I can reach you. As soon as we trap this guy I'll let you know. In the meantime, take care of my angel for me."

"Yeah, I'll do that," Zeke replied, and slowly hung up the phone. He met Angie's gaze. "He wasn't angry with you, was he?"

She smiled. "No, not really. It was good to talk to him. I apologized for running away with you. He said he'd grown used to my impetuous ways." She moved over to where Zeke sat and slid into his lap. "He didn't sound as though he was eager for us to return."

"No, he didn't."

"I wonder why?"

"I suppose he understood that we wanted some time alone."

She nuzzled his chin. "Well, if we aren't going to starve to death, we're going to have to do some shopping. Your poor cupboard is definitely bare."

Zeke also needed to make a private call to Frank. He glanced at his watch. Hugging her to him, he said, "Why don't you make a list of what we need and I'll go to the store. I need to get a haircut, as well." Placing a kiss on the tip of her nose, he said, "You'll probably enjoy having me out from underfoot for a couple of hours.''

She smiled. ''I could never get tired of being with you.''

He came to his feet, still holding her. ''Just keep that thought firmly in mind, Princess, while I show you what a domesticated animal I've become.'' He walked into the kitchen and sat her on the counter. After placing a pad and pencil in her hand, he said, ''Make your list while I go shower.'' He gave her a slow, seductive kiss, pulling her legs around his waist and pressing her tightly against him.

''Are you sure you need to leave right away?'' she whispered, rubbing her breasts against his chest.

He groaned and nibbled at her ear. ''Aren't you hungry?''

She nodded, her eyes bright, then gave him an impish grin. ''But not so hungry I can't wait,'' she admitted a little breathlessly when he dipped his head and nuzzled her breast through her cotton blouse.

Some types of gratification could be postponed, others couldn't, Zeke decided, hauling Angie into his arms once again and heading for the bedroom.

He'd call Frank later.

By the time Angie showered and found something to wear sometime later, Zeke had left. Dreamily she changed the sheets and gathered up their laundry. For the first time since the ceremony, Angie realized that she felt truly married, taking care of domestic chores. Smiling at the idea, she carried the laundry down the hallway to the closet where the washer and dryer were installed.

She couldn't plan any meals until Zeke returned, but she could show him her housewifely skills by dusting and polishing the place. With only one bedroom, the apartment was small enough to be thoroughly cleaned in a relatively short while.

Humming with the current hit music being played on his stereo, Angie found the vacuum cleaner in a cluttered closet in the bedroom and lifted it from between a stack of boxes.

The disruption caused another box to slide off the stack and tumble upside down, dumping its contents around her feet. Stifling a muttered curse, Angie knelt and began to scoop up the mess, then paused when she recognized Zeke's picture on one of the documents.

Puzzled, she examined what looked to be a driver's license, but with someone else's name. The address was unknown, as well. She picked up what looked to be a passport. This, too, had a picture of Zeke, but the name and address listed were different.

Angie stared at the documents scattered around her feet with a sense of numbness. She could feel the heavy beat of her heart in her chest as it sluggishly pounded its rhythm. She forced herself to breathe—to inhale, to exhale—to remember the fundamental functions of her body as her mind began to whirl with questions and images.

She remembered the first time she had seen Zeke, waiting at the Mexico City airport. She remembered her reaction to him, even then. He held a fascination for her that was so strong she hadn't questioned the wisdom of believing him, of trusting him.

He worked for her uncle, didn't he? Her uncle would never have hired someone who wasn't trustworthy. Surely there was a rational explanation for what she had just found.

Was it necessary for Zeke to assume other identities in his job? Quickly she sorted through the various cards and licenses, the passports and visas, trying to make sense out of what she saw.

Was his name really Zeke Daniels?

Did she know the man she was married to?

Angie carefully replaced the scattered pieces of identification in the box, then set the box in the closet. For a moment she stared at the vacuum cleaner as though puzzled by its reason for being there. Then like an automated mannequin she began to clean the apartment, waiting to hear the door open to reveal the man she had married...the stranger she had married...in hopes his explanation could ease the panicky feeling that had swept over her, threatening to consume her.

As soon as Zeke got through to Frank, he asked, "When is the agency going to make their move against De la Garza?"

"I haven't heard, Zeke. Don't tell me you're getting bored with the honeymoon?"

"I've told Angie we'd return to Monterrey, but I don't want her down there when they arrest him."

"Have you told her who you are?"

"No!"

"You've really set yourself up on this one, haven't you?"

Zeke scrubbed his palm across his forehead. "I did what I had to do, Frank. I don't think the man's going to give up easily. I don't want her in danger."

"You know your marrying De la Garza's niece has hurt your credibility with the DEA, don't you? Now they don't know whether they can trust the information you gave them or not."

"Dammit, Frank, you know better than that!"

"They don't."

"Then tell them."

"You may have to do that yourself."

"Fine. Name the time and the place and I'll be there."

There was a pause. "Are you serious?"

"Of course I'm serious!"

"Hold on, I'll see what I can set up."

Canned music played in his ear while Zeke waited. He'd known none of this was going to be easy. Given the paranoia of the intelligence community, he wasn't particularly surprised at their attitude. Well, he didn't really care what they thought. He'd been turned loose to do what he had to do to get the information needed. He'd gotten the damned information. It wasn't anyone's business that he'd also gotten himself married into the family of a drug kingpin.

Lorenzo was just as concerned about protecting Angie as he was. At least he'd give the man that. Maybe this Benito Perez could be traced to—

"Zeke?"

"I'm here."

"All right. We've called a meeting here tomorrow at ten. They're bringing over printouts of everything you turned over. They have some questions maybe you can answer."

"Whatever it takes to get this thing over with. By the way, Frank, tell them to find out whatever they can on a Benito Perez, who may be behind some of the recent trouble Lorenzo's been having. He may be the link we've been looking for. I figure he's someone in the business wanting to take over the De la Garza shipping routes and contacts."

"Was his name on any of the information you gave us?"

"I doubt it. I got it today from Lorenzo."

"You're still in touch with him?"

"Of course. I just married the niece he raised like his own daughter. Hell, Frank! Don't you understand? Angie's all the family he's got left. He's grooming me to take his place once he retires."

"Have you considered the possibility that you may be in over your head, hotshot?"

Zeke sighed. "The thought has occurred to me on one or two occasions, yes."

"I'm not certain whether your decisions have been based on nobility or overactive hormones. Couldn't you have protected the woman without marrying her?"

"Maybe."

"At least you admit to the possibility."

"I've never pretended to be perfect, Frank."

"I've never known you to allow your emotions to get in the way of any of your decisions before, either."

A woman paused outside the telephone booth and peered inside. Zeke nodded to her and said into the phone, "Look, Frank, I've got to get off this phone. I'll see you in your office in the morning."

"Good enough."

"Thanks for your understanding. I know I've been acting out of character. I can't really give a logical explanation of my behavior. Wish I could."

Frank laughed. "Love's never been considered a rational emotion, Zeke. I've always assumed you were immune, that's all."

Zeke hung up the phone and opened the door to the booth, smiling an apology to the woman waiting. She gave him a dazzling smile, but he never noticed. His mind was too busy repeating Frank's last words... love's never been considered a rational emotion... love's never... *Love!*

He stepped outside of the drugstore and leaned against the brick wall for a moment, his shaking knees too weak to hold his weight without some kind of support.

Love?

What was Frank talking about? What did love have to do with the way he'd been feeling... or acting, for that matter? Whatever his feelings, they had nothing in common with such a sappy, sentimental emotion as love.

Frank had really lost it, hadn't he? The guy didn't know what he was talking about.

Somehow, his conclusion about Frank didn't make his knees feel any stronger. Zeke couldn't understand why he was trembling as though suddenly stricken by a fever, or why he had broken out into a cold sweat.

All right. Exactly what was happening here? He wanted Angie. He understood that. His reaction to her was certainly a very basic one. Not only had he found it impossible to keep his hands off her, he'd discovered a strong need to protect her, as well.

But love?

Impossible.

Now he had to face the fact that he hadn't fully thought out how he planned to tell Angie the truth about her uncle. Nor had he considered how she was going to feel toward him when she discovered his role in her uncle's capture.

He had a hunch she was going to hate him.

What did he intend to do about their relationship once she knew the truth? Did he intend to fight to keep what they had together?

For the first time in his life, Zeke felt helpless to control the outcome of a situation that he had set up. He didn't want to think about a life without Angie. He couldn't imagine not having her there in his arms when he fell asleep at night, or cuddled next to him when he awoke each morning.

With his thoughts and emotions in a turmoil, Zeke managed to find his way back to his car. Forgetting about buying groceries, he headed back to the apartment.

He needed to see her. He felt an overwhelming desire to hold her in order to reassure himself that she was real. She had married him, hadn't she? he reminded himself. She must feel something for him. She would understand why he had . . . why it was necessary for him to . . . His thoughts swirled around in his head.

Impatiently weaving his rental car through traffic, Zeke hurried home. He didn't like what he was feeling. He didn't want to feel this vulnerable.

Not with anyone.

Not ever.

He remembered the pain of losing his mother, and later, his best friend. He'd recovered and he'd gone on with his life. He'd also learned that love was too painful to endure when he lost a loved one.

Zeke fought for composure as he locked the car in the underground parking and headed for the elevator that would take him to his apartment. He'd be all right as soon as he saw Angie. Maybe it was time for him to tell her a little about himself, about his background. Maybe he should prepare her for what was going to happen to Lorenzo, to reassure her that he was there for her.

He opened the door of the apartment, only then realizing that he had forgotten to stop for food.

"Angie? Hey, Princess, guess you'd better go with me next time. I forgot all about getting groceries. I got sidetracked and I—" He walked into the living room and saw that she had been cleaning. Everything sparkled. He grinned, the knot in his chest slowly receding.

"Angie?" He walked down the hallway toward the bedroom.

She heard him come in but continued to sit in the rocking chair, which occupied a corner of the bedroom. After she had finished cleaning, Angie had returned to the bedroom and closed the drapes, unwilling to accept the sunshine that poured into the room as though nothing had changed.

Everything had changed. She was lost and adrift in a reality she didn't understand, couldn't begin to comprehend, and had nowhere to turn.

She watched as Zeke paused in the doorway of the bedroom, but she didn't speak. He flipped on the light at the same time he said her name.

"Angie?"

She rocked gently, watching him register surprise, then concern. Seeing him always had such an impact on her. He radiated strength ... and power ... and a charisma that made her quiver.

He crossed the room in long strides. "Are you all right? What's wrong?" He knelt beside her and took her hand between his.

His hands felt warm and she shivered.

This was Zeke. This was the man who had held her, who had loved her, who had protected her. This was the man she loved. Could she pretend that nothing had happened? Was she strong enough to confront him? Was she strong enough to deal with his answers?

"What happened, honey? You're so pale. Did you hurt yourself?" He gave a quick glance around the bedroom. "You've been busy, I can see that. You know you didn't have to do all of the cleaning alone." He took her other hand and held it against his chest.

Angie pulled her hands away. She couldn't think when he touched her. And she knew that she had to think, had to be strong. Taking a deep breath, she said, "Tell me who you are." Her voice wavered slightly. She closed her eyes, no longer able to look at him.

He looked at her blankly. "What are you talking about?"

She forced herself to open her eyes but couldn't look at him. Instead, she studied her hands gripped in her lap. "I found the box in your closet, Zeke. The one with the passports and identifications, with different names and nationalities." She finally met his gaze. "Each of them has your picture on them."

Zeke studied her in silence for a few moments before he answered. She couldn't read anything in his expression now. His eyes had gone dark as though a light had been turned off.

"You know who I am, Angie. I haven't lied to you."

"Then why do you have all those phony IDs? Isn't that illegal?"

"They're part of my job. Technically speaking, they are illegal, I suppose."

"What job? Who do you work for... besides my uncle?"

A muscle jumped in his jaw, but he never dropped his gaze. "I work for the government. I worked in Europe for many years and used several of those aliases."

"Why are you working for my uncle?"

"Because he needed someone like me, someone with my background and expertise."

"Does he know you work for your government?"

"No."

"Then you lied to him."

"I didn't tell him the complete truth."

"If I tell him the truth, what will happen?"

He shrugged and looked away.

"It would cause you problems?"

He sighed. "Yeah, you could say that."

"Will you tell me why you went to work for my uncle?"

"I'm afraid I can't. Not at the moment, anyway."

"You're spying on my uncle, aren't you?" Before he could respond, she said, "Why? Why are you and your government spying on him? What do you think he's done?"

"I can't discuss the matter with you, Angie. I wish I could, but I can't."

"You can't tell me why you were in Mexico?"

He shook his head.

"Is Tio supposed to have done something wrong?"

"Even if he has, whatever he's done has nothing to do with you . . . or with you and me."

She studied him for a long while, trying to make sense out of what he was telling her, wanting desperately to understand. She was frightened. What could Tio have done that would cause the United States government to be interested enough to send Zeke to work for him?

"Why did you marry me?" she finally asked. Angie wasn't at all certain she could face his answer. But she knew that she could no longer pretend that their relationship was what she had originally thought.

"Because I love you, Angie. No other reason." His low voice sounded hoarse.

Oh, how she wanted to believe him! But the doubts had been planted and were rapidly taking root.

She looked around the room. "Why are we in Washington? It isn't because you wanted to spend our honeymoon here, is it?"

"I brought you here because it was the safest place for you to be. Your uncle understands that."

"My uncle's home isn't safe?"

"Have you already forgotten the problems with the plane, the attempted break-ins at the compound? Until we find out who's behind those incidents, then, no, Lorenzo's home isn't safe."

She sighed. "I don't know what to think. My head is spinning. I feel as though I just woke up from a very vivid dream, but one I now know wasn't real at all."

"Angie, if you don't believe anything else, believe this. I love you. I love you more than I've ever loved anyone in my life."

She eyed him uncertainly. "You've never mentioned your feelings for me before."

"No."

She stared at him for a long, silent moment before slowly nodding. "It was never necessary before, I suppose. But now that I've discovered some of your secrets, you feel it necessary to convince me you love me."

"I haven't lied to you, ever. I won't start now. There are just some things that I can't tell you at this time. But they don't have anything to do with us. If you don't want to believe anything else, believe that I've never lied about my feelings for you."

Her head ached with confused thoughts. She didn't know what to think. She knew what she wanted to believe, of course. Like a child, she wanted to continue to believe in happy ever after.

Angie recognized that she was in over her head. Nothing in her life had prepared her for a situation where she had to trust her own judgment so completely. She had relied heavily on her uncle's guidance. She realized...now...that she had trusted Zeke because her uncle trusted him.

But Zeke had lied to her uncle. Zeke was a man with a mysterious background and a mysterious past whose presence in her life was shrouded in more mystery.

Once again her impulsive nature had betrayed her.

She loved Zeke Daniels. There was no doubt in her mind about her feelings for him.

The question was: did she dare trust him?

Ten

"**I** don't believe you!" Zeke growled, slapping his hand on the top of the desk for emphasis. "I don't care what your so-called experts tell you, I was there, dammit! I know what I saw! Of course this man's running an illegal operation, and the records I turned in should prove that fact!"

Zeke sat at a conference table with five of the men involved in the drug trafficking problems on the Texas-Mexico border. The head of the operation had just summarized their findings with regard to the files belonging to Lorenzo De la Garza.

"All right, Zeke, I can understand your irritation and frustration. All of us were shocked at what turned up on those reports. I'll admit that we thought at first you might have decided to protect him since you married into the family." He paused when he saw the sudden flash of fire in Zeke's eyes. In a more conciliatory tone, he added, "We ran them through cryptology, we did everything possible to make certain they weren't in some kind of code. What we discovered was that the data is exactly what it looks like—meticulous business records for De la Garza's operation...and it's all legal." The man leaned back in his chair, tapping his pencil. "Naturally, we've been stunned by this evidence, since we've put so much time into proving his participation in drug trafficking. What did you see while you were there that makes you believe we've misinterpreted our findings?"

"His life-style, for one thing. The man lives like royalty. Where else would he be getting that kind of money, if not from drugs? He's got his own plane, he has an army of security men around him at all times, he's got the perfect cover to hide behind—his factories where he's supposedly manufacturing goods for export."

"Yes, we know all of that, Zeke. His investments are definitely paying off for him. What I'm asking is, did you ever see any drugs? Did you ever see a transaction where money and drugs were exchanged?"

"Of course not! The man wasn't going to trust me to sit in on something that sensitive. He's too smart for that."

"Didn't you say he used you not only to beef up his security system but as his personal bodyguard, as well? Didn't you travel with him?"

"Yes."

"Were there times when he had you stay behind while he went somewhere alone?"

"No. But I was only there a couple of months."

"Two months is a long time in the drug business. You would have seen something during that time."

"I identified two undercover agents! Don't forget that!"

"But were they on his payroll?"

"They were working for him... yeah."

"Doing what?"

Zeke paused, rubbing his forehead. He had a head-ache that wouldn't quit. He hadn't gotten much sleep last night, lying there beside Angie, wondering how he was going to break the news to her that her uncle was involved in running drugs. He also dreaded to tell her his part in the operation.

Now he was being told that Lorenzo De la Garza was *not* the head of a drug cartel, that he was exactly what he represented himself to be, a highly success-ful, very rich businessman who was having trouble with a particularly nasty business rival who was try-ing to stop him in any way he could.

One of Benito Perez's ploys had been to report Lorenzo De la Garza as a member of a drug running cartel. What was now suspected was that Perez had managed to plant drugs in one of Lorenzo's factory shipments, then Perez tipped off the border patrol to make sure the drugs were discovered. The amounts found were enough to encourage the assignment of an all-out surveillance team. When nothing positive was reported back from those assigned to the case, Zeke had become involved.

He thought about the agents he had identified. "All right, I see what you mean. One of the agents worked as a yardman, the other one helped in the kitchen."

"Exactly. They were employees, much like you were. They were paid a wage of sorts, but it wasn't enough to tempt anyone into hiding information."

Zeke shook his head. "So you're telling me that the large-scale, multidepartmental operation designed to flush this guy out in the open managed to find out that he hasn't done anything wrong?"

"He may be doing all kinds of things that are wrong, Daniels," Frank put in. "Just nothing to do with drugs. The man is a financial wizard."

"His records were impeccable," the head of the operation pointed out. "He knows where every peso goes, he knows how and where it comes in. At any given time he has an exact idea where he stands monetarily."

Zeke dropped his head in his hands. His head was swimming. How could he have been so wrong about a man? How could not just one, but *two* intelligence departments be so wrong about a man?

"Well, he certainly made us all look like fools," he murmured.

"Actually, we managed to do that without his help. As far as he knows, the yardman found a better job, the kitchen help had a sick mother."

"What about me?"

"Good question. How did you leave? Did you give notice or did you walk out?"

"I eloped with his niece. He's expecting us back home once he deals with this Perez character."

"Then he has no way of knowing that you were working for us. I doubt that he knows you copied the files. We certainly haven't leaked any of the information. I'll admit to a few red faces in our department over this. We've been after the man for almost three years. Three years! This type of news is exactly what we don't want getting out to the press corps—how we're spending the taxpayer's money!"

Another one of the men spoke up. "But we also follow up every lead we're given and the situation looked suspicious to us. Of course it was supposed to. We were shown just enough to whet our appetite, thinking we were on to something."

"It looks like the joke's on me, gentlemen," Zeke said slowly, leaning back in his chair. "Mr. Lorenzo De la Garza has plans to groom me to take over his operation when he retires. I thought he meant the drug trade. I can't believe I so completely misread a situation."

"Don't be too hard on yourself, Zeke," Frank offered after a moment. "We're trained to look for ulterior motives, for cover-ups, for illicit practices."

"Even when none exist!" Zeke replied. He still had to look at all the implications where he was concerned. What was he supposed to do now?

He could go back to Mexico. He could quit this job and work for Lorenzo for real. He could go back to Angie and explain that—

Explain that he had been gathering evidence to put her uncle behind bars only to discover there wasn't any evidence to be found?

Not likely.

"Zeke?"

He looked at Frank. "You did a hell of a job for us. I believe your explanations today have given us a clearer picture of the situation. I think we'll let this terminate your part of the operation. If you decide to take Lorenzo's offer, I'll certainly understand. After all, you're part of his family now. Whatever you decide, let me know, all right?"

Zeke pushed his chair back from the table and stood. "I can't say I'm sorry about the outcome of the investigation, gentlemen, given my circumstances. Angie would have been devastated with news of her uncle's involvement in illegal shipments of any kind."

Frank stuck out his hand. "At least now we have a new lead. I'll see what happens when we place Benito Perez under a magnifying glass."

Zeke shook Frank's hand, nodded to the other men and left the room. He'd go back to Angie and tell her what had been happening. He had a hunch that Perez would soon have his hands full with other problems and wouldn't have the time or resources to continue to harass Lorenzo.

Zeke felt as though a huge weight had been lifted off his shoulders. He could make whatever explanations he had to, then get on with his new life. If necessary he would spend the rest of his life convincing Angie that he loved her.

He was looking forward to that particular assignment.

"Angie?" he called as soon as he opened the door to the apartment.

There was no answer. He strode down the hallway. "Angie, honey, where are you?"

The bedroom was empty. So was the dresser where she had placed a few of her possessions. A sudden pain caught him in the region of his heart when he noticed that the only item on the dresser was an envelope with his name written on it. A sense of foreboding made him hesitate before he picked up the envelope and opened it. Folded sheets of paper lay inside. Fumbling them open, he read:

"Zeke, I've taken the coward's way out, I know, but my feelings for you are too strong to be able to tell you in person that I have decided to leave.

I don't know why you were working for Tio, but I feel you and your government were hoping to find him doing something wrong. I believe that you used my feelings for you for your own purposes, so that you would have a bargaining tool against my uncle.

For everyone's sake I've decided to return to Monterrey. I don't want to be a part of whatever you are involved in. I love my uncle too much to ever allow my impulsive decisions to hurt him.

I hope you will be able to forgive me someday. If you wish to have our marriage annulled, I will agree to whatever necessary. I'll wait to hear from you.

                                                    Angela

Zeke sank onto the side of the bed and stared at the feminine handwriting. A part of his mind refused to take in the contents of the letter, focusing on the neat penmanship instead. He'd never seen her writing before. There was so much he didn't know about her.

She loved her uncle. That much he knew. She would never forgive Zeke for what he had attempted to do. Somewhere deep inside he had known that, as well.

What did he intend to do now? Ignoring his feelings for the moment, he knew that he had originally whisked her away from Mexico in an attempt to protect her. She no longer needed his protection.

She no longer needed to be married to him.

He could go back and attempt to explain, or he could accept her decision to get out of his life. He knew what he wanted to do, but for the first time in his life, Zeke discovered he didn't have the courage to face the possible outcome. His feelings for her were too strong to face her when she told him she no longer wanted to be a part of his life.

Zeke stretched out across the bed and closed his eyes. He concentrated on blanking out the memories. He needed every ounce of energy he could summon to help him to forget.

How long would it take for him to recover from the self-inflicted wound of loving Angela De la Garza Daniels?

"Would you care for something to drink, Ms. De la Garza?" the flight attendant asked Angie, drawing her out of her reverie.

Angie glanced up from the magazine she'd been mindlessly studying and attempted to smile at the friendly woman who was being so solicitous to her first-class passengers.

"Thank you, no."

After the woman moved away, Angie dropped the magazine to her lap and stared out the window of the plane. Now that she was on her way to Mexico, there was no turning back. She had to come to grips with what she had done. Tio would want some kind of explanation for her inexplicable behavior. She had so little excuse for her impulsiveness this time. What could she say?

The one thing she knew for certain was that somehow she was going to have to stop running and face the consequences of the decisions she had made in the past few weeks.

Although Tio had strongly resisted the idea of her coming to Mexico at this time, she had come anyway, determined to share with him her dreams of starting a school in the village, of making her home permanently in Mexico. She'd never gotten around to telling him about all her detailed plans. Instead, she'd allowed her instant attraction to Zeke to distract her from her goal. Oblivious to the inherent dangers of becoming intimate with a man she barely knew, she had thrown herself headlong into a relationship.

She had trusted Zeke because she trusted Tio's judgment. What she hadn't taken into consideration was that Tio's trust in the man had to do with his profession, not as a prospective member of the family.

She'd been such a fool... immature, impossibly naive, and irresponsible.

She recognized that at the moment she not only was running from Zeke, she was running from herself, which was certainly an exercise in futility. She sighed, rubbing her hand across her forehead where a throbbing ache had found a seemingly permanent home.

There was no one to save her this time from her impulsive choices. Neither man in her life could rescue her. She had placed herself in a situation that needed to be looked at with maturity, a trait she feared was truly lacking in her makeup.

Fact: she was now married to a man who worked for a foreign government while ostensibly working for her uncle.

Fact: he would not tell her why, an ominous lack of trust.

Fact: she had walked out on a week-old marriage because she didn't know how to handle being a wife.

The question she had to face at this time was what did she do now? Should she warn her uncle of Zeke's dual occupation? If she did, would she be placing Zeke in a possibly dangerous situation? Loyalty to one man could be disloyalty to the other. Did she owe Zeke her loyalty, regardless of their legal tie? He had lied by omitting to tell her some important information about himself, information that might harm Tio.

She closed her eyes, wishing for the wisdom of Solomon to know what to do now. How could she consider staying married to a man who lived in another country when all she could dream about these past few years was to get back home to Mexico? She'd easily responded to Zeke's suggestion to marry when she thought that he would continue to work for Tio there in Mexico. It was another thing entirely to think about living in Washington, D.C., while her husband traveled, leaving her alone.

What she had finally admitted to herself earlier in the day was that she wasn't ready for marriage. Unfortunately for everyone concerned, she had left the discovery of that particular insight a little late. Acknowledging this latest piece of awareness had, if possible, dropped her self-esteem another notch down on her personal evaluation scale...causing her to teeter dangerously close to self-loathing.

So where did she go from here, besides flying home to throw herself into Tio's arms? She'd messed up in a really big way, with no idea what to do next.

When the plane reached Dallas, Angie had a two-hour layover. She called her uncle to tell him she was on her way home and to ask him to meet her plane.

"Is Zeke with you?"

"No, Tio. I'm alone."

"But why? Isn't it customary for a couple to honeymoon together?"

"I've left him, Tio. I should never have run off with him like this." She bit her bottom lip, hard, to gain some control over her emotions.

"What did he do to you?" Lorenzo demanded to know.

"It's more like what I did to him. I trapped him into marrying me, then didn't have the courage to live with my actions."

"What do you mean, you trapped him? What's going on with you two?"

"I'll explain everything when I get home, Tio. I promise. I hadn't realized until these past few days how very childish I've been, wanting whatever attracted me without regard to whether it was good for me or not...or if I could handle the consequences. I've discovered that I've made a lot of mistakes recently. Now I've got to face each one of them and do what I can to find a solution."

"I don't understand what you're talking about, but we'll discuss it further when you arrive."

"Yes, Tio. Thank you for being there for me." She hung up before her voice could break.

In the following weeks Angie spent most of her time alone. She took long walks, she visited the village and talked with the mothers, she discussed some of her ideas about a preschool with her uncle.

She made no attempt to contact Zeke. Not that she didn't want to talk with him...to hear his voice again. Not that she didn't miss him with every aching breath she drew. No, she didn't call because she didn't know what to say to him.

She had hoped that he would contact her, that he would in some way open the line of communication between them so that she could attempt an explanation of some of the things she had discovered about herself.

Regardless of her confusion, she knew with a deep certainty that she loved Zeke with every fiber of her being. When he didn't call or return to Mexico, she knew that she had blown any chance she might have had to apologize to him for her behavior.

Angie lost track of the many letters she had written to him, then had torn up. How could she begin to excuse her inexcusable behavior?

She tried to imagine what he was doing now, wondering if he was still in Washington or whether he had returned overseas to work once again.

It was time to pick up the various pieces of her life and get on with what she had to do to survive the emotional backlash of her impulsive behavior.

Zeke rolled over with a groan, burying his head under his pillow to muffle the steady pounding. Why didn't whoever was trying to beat down his door go away?

He'd lost track of time since Angie had left. Days and nights had run meaninglessly together. He'd managed to go to the store and buy some food and several bottles of his favorite brand of bourbon. The bourbon was for medicinal purposes . . . to help him create amnesia.

Unfortunately the damn stuff wasn't doing the job.

He'd unplugged the phone two . . . maybe three . . . days ago. He didn't want to talk to anybody. He didn't want to see anybody. He just wished the jerk hammering on his door would give up and go somewhere else.

The steady pounding continued, despite the muffling effect of the pillow.

"All right, all right!" he finally muttered, throwing the pillow across the room and rising. His head kept a pounding counterpart to the noise on the front door. He fumbled for his jeans and drew them up to his waist. They hung loosely, reminding him that he'd been skipping a few meals lately.

The room was dark, which didn't mean much since he'd kept the drapes pulled. He had no idea what day it was, or what time it was. He didn't much care.

Rather than turn on a light, he felt his way along the hallway until he reached the front door.

He attempted to peer through the security peephole but couldn't focus. He finally gave it up. "Who is it?" he demanded gruffly through the door.

"Lorenzo."

Zeke blinked in disbelief. Lorenzo? He fumbled with the lock and jerked the door open in disbelief. His former employer stood before him, nattily dressed as always, looking as though he was prepared to camp in the hallway if necessary.

"Are you the one who's been making all that racket?" His puzzlement slightly softened his distinctly hostile tone. But not by much.

"May I come in?" Lorenzo asked politely.

"Why?" was the bald response.

Lorenzo's mouth twitched slightly. "Because I prefer talking to you somewhere other than the hallway—" he glanced around him "—private though it may seem at the moment."

Zeke ran his hand through his hair, shook his head in an attempt to clear it, then shrugged and stepped away from the door. "Come in, if you want," he said, turning away. "I'll be back in a minute."

It took longer than a minute for him to shower and shave, but he needed the time to adjust to his unexpected company, to get awake, and to prepare himself to face whatever Lorenzo had felt was important enough to come to Washington to tell him.

He looked at the bloodshot eyes of the man in the mirror and shook his head in disgust. He looked like hell. He hadn't shaved in days and winced as he nicked himself, wondering if he'd forgotten how to shave. He reminded himself that there was no need to hurry. Obviously Lorenzo didn't intend to go anywhere until he'd said his piece.

Zeke grabbed a towel and gingerly patted his face dry. He combed his wet hair, noticing that he needed a haircut. Then he went into the bedroom and found a clean shirt hanging in the closet. The shirt and a clean pair of jeans made him feel almost human again.

Without bothering to search for socks or shoes he headed toward the living room, pausing in the doorway. Lorenzo stood at the window looking out. Without turning around, he said, "Nice view of the city."

Zeke glanced out the window, finally registering the blackness outside. He went into the kitchen area that was separated from the living room by a bar. "You want some coffee?" he asked, reaching for the canister.

Lorenzo turned and nodded. "Yes, thank you."

"When did you get in?"

"Yesterday. I've been trying to reach you for several days now, but there was no answer." He glanced around the room and saw the phone sitting on a side table, unplugged. "I'm beginning to understand why."

Zeke made no comment. He measured coffee and water as though no one else were around.

"You look like hell, Zeke," Lorenzo finally said.

Zeke glanced up, his gaze meeting Lorenzo's briefly before he looked away. He reached for a couple of coffee mugs, filled and carried them into the living room. After offering one to Lorenzo, he sat down in the large overstuffed chair.

"So how did you find me?" he finally asked.

Lorenzo sat down on the sofa across from him and leaned back with a sigh. "It wasn't easy. I had to go over your résumé and call some of the numbers listed. It took me two days until I was finally connected to Frank Carpenter."

Zeke had been staring at his coffee during Lorenzo's explanation, but glanced up in surprise at the mention of Frank's name. He straightened in the chair. "Frank told you where I lived?"

Lorenzo smiled. "Is it supposed to be a secret?"

Not a secret, exactly, but Frank was notoriously closemouthed about things. He strictly adhered to the "need to know" policy in the business. "I'm just surprised."

"I went to his office this morning in hopes of getting some clarity on the situation."

"What situation?"

"On your showing up to work for me, then not returning."

Zeke relaxed into his chair once more and drawled, "I hope he gave you what you were looking for."

He was taken by surprise once again when Lorenzo nodded. "He helped me to see the big picture. Actually, he was a great deal of help. He gave me enough solid evidence on Benito Perez to turn him over to authorities when I return home. He said it was the least he could do since I had paid the salary for the man who obtained the information. I understand he was part of my kitchen help." Lorenzo's smile was filled with self-mockery. "I owe your government for their help in getting that particular matter resolved."

"Frank was a regular chatterbox, wasn't he?" Zeke muttered, shaking his head.

"Under the circumstances, he felt your organization owed me more than an apology for their infiltrating my operation. I'll admit that being able to rid myself of Perez goes a long way to placate my anger at the loss of my privacy."

"I'm sure Frank appreciated your viewing the matter in such a positive light." Zeke took another sip from his coffee, slowly feeling the caffeine work its magic in his body.

"I'm a businessman, Zeke. I don't have to like a situation to understand why it was necessary. I had no idea I was under suspicion for distributing drugs. When you first appeared, my only concern was that you weren't planted there by my adversary." He paused to drink from his cup before continuing. "Once I discovered your background, I knew you wouldn't have been recruited to sabotage my business. It never occurred to me that I was your target."

The coffee helped to clear Zeke's head. He went back to the kitchen and returned with the carafe, refilling both cups.

Once he sat down again, Lorenzo said, "You were a great help to me, Zeke. I want you to know that. Regardless of the reason you hired out to me, I owe you a debt of gratitude…not only for the way you set up the new security system, but also the way you took care of Angela."

Zeke flinched at the mention of the name he had known would eventually become part of their conversation. "Oh, I took care of her, all right," he muttered into his cup before draining half its contents.

Lorenzo sighed. "What's between you and Angela is none of my business, I know, but when two people I care about are so desperately unhappy, I feel it imperative to do whatever I can to help."

Zeke eyed the man across from him. "Are you implying I'm desperately unhappy about something?" His gruff voice once again had an edge of hostility.

"I've seen you in better shape than this," Lorenzo replied.

"I'm on my own time now, doing what I want to do."

"Which is?"

Zeke shrugged. "Resting between assignments."

"Ah." Lorenzo set his cup down and made a steeple with his fingers. "Then you don't intend to return to Monterrey to learn my business?"

Zeke stared at him in disbelief. "You mean you still want me to work with you?"

"Yes."

Zeke couldn't think of anything to say about this totally unexpected development. After a moment he shook his head abruptly, his laugh sounding harsh and unamused. "Right. I can just see how that would work."

"Why wouldn't it?"

His irritation at his need to explain was echoed in his voice. "I have no intention of going anywhere near Angie."

"Why?"

Zeke scowled at the other man's obtuseness. "Why?" he repeated, his voice rising. "In case she hasn't mentioned it to you, she wants no part of me or our hasty marriage. She's convinced I was just using her to get to you."

"Were you?" Lorenzo asked mildly.

"Hell, no! I didn't *need* to use her for anything. I was already set up with you before she ever showed up." Unable to sit still, Zeke sprang from his chair and began to pace. "What was going on with us had nothing to do with the job I was hired to do, either for you or the government!"

"Did you ever explain that to her?" Lorenzo asked in the same mild manner.

"Ha! She never gave me a chance! She jumped to all kinds of conclusions—" he turned and glared at Lorenzo "—most of which were wrong, I might add. Just because I couldn't tell her the truth about why I was there, she decided she couldn't trust me." He stalked over to the bar and poured himself a double shot of bourbon. "Which is fine with me!" He lifted the glass to his mouth.

"I can see that," Lorenzo quietly replied. "Is that why you've crawled into that bottle, because you don't care that your new wife doesn't trust you?"

Zeke lowered the glass and glared at Lorenzo. "I never asked her to trust me."

"Maybe you should have."

"Maybe I should have done a lot of things that I didn't do." He glanced distastefully at the full glass he

held in his hand and slammed it down, spinning away
from the bar and going to stand in front of the window. "I sure as hell know I *did* a lot of things that I
shouldn't have. But you don't have to worry, I'm
paying for every damn one of them!"

"I'm really surprised at you, Zeke. You never struck
me as the kind of man to sit around and sulk."

Zeke stiffened, feeling the steadily building rage
within threatening to break through. Sulk? The man
had the audacity to accuse him of some infantile attitude when he— Slowly he turned to look at Lorenzo,
who was comfortably leaning back on the sofa,
watching him.

"Is that what you think?" Zeke managed to say
between his clenched teeth.

"What I think is that you have the opportunity of
a lifetime to come in and learn my business with the
idea that you will take over when I retire, and that you
would prefer to throw that opportunity away rather
than face one rather petite individual and tell her the
truth about yourself and the job you were hired to
do."

"Why should I waste my time? The conclusion she
jumped to, while not really right, isn't nearly as bad as
the fact that I was actively gathering evidence to put
her beloved uncle behind bars. I don't consider my
unwillingness to beat a dead horse the same thing as
sulking."

"I see. It's lack of courage, then?"

"You know, Lorenzo, you're really beginning to ir-
ritate me," Zeke replied in a menacing understate-
ment of his mood.

Lorenzo's grin was filled with humor. "God, I hope
so! It beats that whipped-dog look you wore when I

first laid eyes on you. What's wrong with feeling some honest anger?''

Zeke couldn't believe what he was hearing. ''You mean you've been deliberately provoking me?''

''Something like that. More like pulling the tiger's tail in an effort to wake you up.''

''I'm awake, you son of a—'' Zeke threw up his hands and turned away.

''Angie's dealing with her own pain, you know.''

''Good for Angie,'' Zeke threw over his shoulder, looking at the lights of D.C.

''What happened between the two of you happened very quickly. That doesn't mean that it was any less real than a long-term courtship. I'm doubly impressed that you removed her from danger, even more so when I realize you thought some of the danger might be generated by me.''

''Oh, yeah. I just barged right in, in my shiny savior suit, and carried her off on my trusty steed.''

''You did what you thought best in a dangerous situation.''

''Good for me. Sainthood is the logical next step, wouldn't you say?''

Lorenzo laughed. ''Somehow I don't think we have to worry about that just yet.''

Without turning around, Zeke muttered, ''I'm real glad you find me so damned amusing.''

Silence settled in the room and for several minutes Lorenzo found no reason to interrupt it. Eventually he said, ''You've never been in love before, have you?''

''Who says I'm in love?'' Zeke said to the window.

''It's a scary place to be. I for one have always run whenever I found myself in danger of falling in love. I have a hunch you would have run, as well, if you hadn't been committed to doing your job. As I see it, you have a couple of options. You can use Angie's leaving you as an excuse to not have to deal with these new and very confusing feelings you're experiencing, or you can face up to them, deal with them, and do whatever you can to make your relationship with her work.''

Zeke didn't say anything.

''So.'' Lorenzo stood. ''I have done what I came to Washington to do. My good judgment in hiring you has been confirmed. My offer to keep you on the payroll has been extended. Whatever you decide from here is up to you.''

Zeke didn't turn around.

''I can let myself out,'' Lorenzo added, heading toward the door. He opened the door and looked at the man standing with his back to the room. ''Thanks for the coffee . . . and good luck, whatever you decide.'' Quietly he closed the door behind him.

Zeke continued to stare out the window, relieved to be alone once again.

Lorenzo might be a wizard in the business world, but he knew nothing about relationships. Oh, he was good at dishing out advice, but he'd never bothered to commit himself to a woman.

Zeke's mistake was in marrying Angie in the first place. Why had he been so quixotic? There had been no reason to—

Wait a minute. Hadn't he argued the point that she could be pregnant? Hadn't he wanted to protect her in case their lovemaking had—

How could he have forgotten? Would she tell him if she was pregnant? Maybe she wouldn't want to be around the father of her child, even if she were pregnant.

He could call and talk with her. He could ask her point-blank if she was going to have his child. Lorenzo couldn't be more wrong in his observations. He wasn't sulking and he certainly wasn't a coward.

He just couldn't remember a time in his life when he'd felt so much pain.

Eleven

He found his car in the long-term parking lot at the McAllen airport. It would probably cost him a fortune to pay the charges, but there was no reason to abandon the car he'd bought when he first returned to Texas several months ago.

Zeke had spent several miserable days in his apartment in an effort to forget or ignore Lorenzo's comments, but in the end he knew that Lorenzo was right.

He was a coward.

From the time he'd first met Angie, he'd had difficulty keeping his hands off her. Now that he knew exactly how she felt in his arms, he was afraid that not even with his renowned self-control could he handle being in her presence without grabbing her and insisting that she forgive him.

He hated to admit that he'd been hiding in his apartment like some animal in his lair, licking his wounds. Whether he liked the idea or not, he knew that he had to face Angie and tell her exactly what he had done and why.

He'd rather face the KGB any day.

He crossed into Mexico a little after one o'clock and headed south. Despite the danger inherent in the many assignments he'd covered over the years, he had never experienced such a gut-level dread. He hated what he was feeling because he felt so helpless. His future was all wrapped up in the hands of the woman he'd been unable to resist from the time he'd first seen a photograph of her.

He resented her control over his life, but his resentment couldn't take away the love he felt for her.

By the time he reached Lorenzo's compound, he felt grim. A brief glance into the car mirror revealed that he looked just like he felt. The guard at the gate grinned and waved him inside. Once he parked the car in front of the house, his jaw was clenched and his muscles taut.

He stood by the car and stretched, deciding not to remove his aviator sunglasses. His eyes still looked like road maps with their multitude of red lines. Zeke took a deep breath and walked to the front door. It opened after his first rap.

"H'lo, Freddie," he said to the man who had opened the door. "Good to see you again."

"Zeke! Hey, welcome back. It's great to see you, man. We've missed you around here."

Zeke nodded. "I had some business to take care of. You know how it is."

"Sure, sure. Just glad you're back. Lorenzo's in his office."

"Oh. Well, uh—thanks."

He supposed he needed to tell Lorenzo that he was back. He started down the hallway and was even with the salon doorway when he saw movement inside. He glanced into the room and froze. Angie was arranging flowers at one of the tables, flowers she'd obviously just brought inside from the courtyard, since the French doors stood open.

He drank in the sight of her, his eyes darting quickly to trace her profile from her head to her feet. She looked thinner than he'd ever seen her...and pale. His breath caught in his throat. Was she ill?

Still hovering in the doorway, he said, "Hello, Angie," in a quiet voice.

She spun around with a muffled cry, knocking some of the flowers to the floor.

"Zeke!"

Now that she was facing him, he could see the dark smudges beneath her eyes. He walked into the room, stopping a few feet from her. "How have you been?"

She rested her hand on her chest. He could see a tremor in her fingers. "I didn't know you were coming," was all she said in reply.

"Didn't you? I figure we have some things to discuss."

Her eyes widened slightly, and he realized that his tone sounded menacing. He glanced around. "Could we sit down somewhere?" *Before you fall down,* he wanted to add. This close he could see that she was shaking.

She edged over to one of the nearby chairs and sat. He pulled another one near so that they sat facing each other. "Are you afraid of me?" he demanded.

Angie looked surprised. "Of course not. I've never been afraid of you."

"So why are you shaking in your boots like the bogeyman just walked into the room?"

She dropped her head, but he saw the slight tilt of her lips and the slight relaxing of her shoulders. "You surprised me, that's all. Why didn't you tell me you were coming?"

He thought about that for a moment, then gave a gusty sigh. "All right. I promised that I would tell you everything. That I wouldn't lie about anything, okay? The truth is I was afraid if I told you I was coming, you wouldn't be here when I arrived."

She looked taken back. "Oh."

He ran his hand through his hair, trying to remember what he had planned to tell her, trying to remember how he had planned to tell her.

His first words were, "Are you all right? You've lost weight."

She clasped her hands in front of her, resting them on her knees. "I'm all right. I just haven't been eating much."

"Do you know if—I mean, has it been long enough to know whether you are—uh—"

She rescued him by answering his unspoken concern. "I don't know, actually. I suppose there is that possibility, but everything in my life's been so chaotic... and I've been so upset that it could just be nerves."

"Aren't there tests you could take?"

"I suppose. I guess I wasn't ready to find out, one way or the other."

"Oh." Well, that certainly didn't tell him much. "Did Lorenzo tell you he came to see me?" he finally asked.

She glanced up from where she had been intently studying her clasped hands. "Yes."

Angie was certainly being a fount of information today. He reached over and took her hands and held them. They felt as though she'd had them submersed in a mountain stream. He stroked them, willing her not to withdraw them. She raised her head and met his gaze.

"I, uh, need to explain what was going on when we met. I finally got clearance to tell you."

"Clearance?"

"Yeah."

"From your government?"

"That's right."

She tugged her hands free and returned them to their nesting place in her lap.

"Dammit, Angie, will you at least give me a chance to explain?" He came to his feet in a lunge and strode over to the French doors. It had been a stupid idea to think he could get her to listen or to understand.

As though responding to his thoughts, she said, "I'm listening, Zeke."

He spun around and faced her. She looked more composed somehow, and her cheeks were tinted with becoming color. Why did she have to be so damned beautiful? He hated feeling so vulnerable, absolutely hated it!

Taking a deep breath, he slowly exhaled and forced himself to sit down once again. "All right. I can see where you felt that I'd lied to you, but I haven't. I really haven't. Everything I told you about myself and my life was true. The work in Europe was for the government. I did a great deal of covert stuff for years, but with all the changes over there I was recalled to

Washington. Then I was loaned to another agency to work down here in an attempt to stop the flow of drug trafficking along the border.''

"You thought Tio was involved in drugs."

He heard the certainty in her voice and asked, "Did he tell you that?"

She nodded.

"Then you understand why I was working for him?"

"He told me what he'd found out while he was in Washington. He's grateful that you and your government helped him to deal with the threats on his life and his property." She lifted her chin and faced him. "He reminded me that you saved my life with your flying skills. I already knew that."

Zeke watched her warily. "Then you already know everything I've come here to say. Does any of this make a difference to you? I mean, do you still want to end our marriage?"

She stared at him for an endless time, searching his face, seeing the pain there. "I never wanted our marriage to end, Zeke."

"But you walked out."

"I know. I don't think I can find the words to explain. I was hurt... and confused... and unprepared to face the reality of our situation." She shook her head, impatient with her inability to find the necessary words that would help her. Restless, she stood and walked over to the window. "I've been such a child, in so many ways," she said without looking at him. "I've led such a sheltered life that I've never been emotionally involved with anyone before. I was totally unprepared to handle my strong reaction to you when we met." She turned and faced him. "Everything happened so quickly between us. I was caught up in something so new and so wonderful that I never thought about where it was all heading.'' Angie walked back to where he sat and sank down into her chair once more. ''I realize that you married me because you wanted to protect me. What I didn't realize at the time was that I needed protection from myself most of all.''

''Don't you think you're being a little hard on yourself?''

''Am I?''

''Yeah, I think so. I mean, if we could all function as nonfeeling intellectuals, using only logic and reason, we'd probably grow pointed ears and hail Vulcan as our home planet.'' He reached over and took her hand. ''What have you done that you feel is so bad?''

She forced herself to meet his gaze. ''Walking out on you certainly wasn't the most mature move I've ever made.''

''I don't know about mature. It certainly created a great deal of pain and from what I can tell, the pain wasn't all on my side.''

''That's my point. I was so wrapped up in my own feelings that I didn't give a thought to how you'd react when you came home and found me gone.''

Zeke looked away. ''Something tells me Lorenzo had a few tales to relate about me when he got home.''

''He said I hurt you badly.''

Zeke shrugged without answering.

''You are the very last person I would want to hurt, Zeke. I knew I wouldn't be able to talk, even if I attempted to call you. I knew that as soon as I heard your voice I would break down. After that I tried to write and tell you what was in my heart, but it was hopeless.''

"I'm here now, Princess. Can you tell me what you want to do about us?''

"When do you have to go back?''

"I don't. I've resigned the Washington job. Lorenzo offered me a place in his organization while he was there. I'm seriously considering it.''

"But you haven't made a final decision.''

He shook his head. "No. I couldn't continue to live here and see you on a daily basis if I didn't know I would go to sleep every night with you in my arms.''

"You're very forgiving.''

"No. Just realistic. I agree that you and I got too involved too quickly. I willingly accept the blame for that because I'm old enough... and experienced enough... to know better. Once we'd been together, I couldn't keep my hands off you. The best damage control, under those particular circumstances, was to marry you.'' He gave her an endearingly lopsided smile. "Nothing's really changed, you know. I'm having trouble sitting here right now when all I want to do is to haul you upstairs and love the daylights out of you.''

"As though nothing's wrong between us?''

"Well, the way I figure it is, if we love each other enough, we've got the rest of our lives together to work out all the details. I'm sure this won't be the only time we get crossways with each other. All I'm asking is that you don't walk away from the problem. Is that too much to ask?''

Angie slid to her knees beside his chair. "Oh, Zeke, I love you so much!'' She put her arms around him. With little effort he pulled her onto his lap. They sat there holding each other, each regretting the pain inflicted on the other, each silently vowing to make up for their past actions.

"Well, it looks as though you two have made up," Lorenzo said, striding into the room. "I just got word that you arrived, Daniels. Are you ready to go to work, or are you just visiting?"

Before Zeke could answer, Angie said, "He's here to stay, Tio. But don't plan to put him to work immediately." She smiled into Zeke's eyes. "I have some plans of my own for the next few days that will occupy most of his time."

Zeke glanced up at Lorenzo's startled expression, then down to his wife, whose saucy response was accompanied by a beautiful blush.

"Looks like I've found myself a new boss," Zeke said with a grin, hugging her even tighter. "I'll do my best to make you both happy, no matter how long it takes!"

Lorenzo laughed, shook his head and walked out of the room, saying, "You've definitely got your job cut out for you."

Zeke glanced down at Angie and grinned. "Maybe so, but I sure do like all of the fringe benefits."

He picked her up and started for the stairs.

Epilogue

Zeke picked up the phone on the first ring and heard a voice from his past...from another lifetime...greet him.

"Frank! You ol' son of a gun. How've you been?"

"Working to keep myself alive. I hadn't talked with you in some time. Thought I'd give you a call to see if you were bored with the business world, yet."

Zeke laughed. "Believe me, my old life was tame compared to what goes on at some of these board meetings. I've wondered at times if I was going to get out in one piece."

"And you love it, right?"

"Yeah, I guess I've always been a sucker for a challenge."

"How's Angela?"

"She's doing very well these days, considering."

"Considering what?"

"Well, she's expecting . . . again."

"My God, Zeke, it's a wonder you have *time* for business. What do the girls and Ty think about the new addition?"

"We haven't told them, yet. We still have a few months to break the news."

"But four kids in five years, Zeke!"

"I know, Frank. I know. I, uh, well, we didn't exactly plan it this way, we just seem to—what I mean is, we, uh—"

"Hey, man, you don't have to explain to me. I get the picture." His amusement was obvious, which wasn't surprising. Zeke still had trouble seeing himself as a family man, but he was certainly enjoying every aspect of family life.

Frank's voice sobered when he continued. "I wanted to pass on an official acknowledgment and appreciation for what you've been doing. You've passed on some very useful information over the years that's been very helpful to us. We just picked off a well-established ring down there this week."

"I read about the bust in the paper. I'm pleased I could help you."

"You know, Zeke, a couple of times you've made the local agents look like amateurs. You've managed to obtain information they've been after for years."

"We have developed a helluva network here, Frank. We sort through all kinds of information on a daily basis. It helps us stay in business. If some of it can help you, it doesn't cost me anything to pass it on."

"I was told to give you an official word of thanks and offer whatever payment you needed."

"I don't need or want payment. I've told you that more than once."

"I know. Just doing what I'm told."

"Good enough, Frank. Glad you called."

"If you ever get up this way, I'd enjoy visiting with you."

"I'm surprised you're still around," Zeke replied, grinning. "I figured the whole complex would have been sold by now."

"Don't I wish! I wouldn't mind retiring, myself. Well, hang in there. Give my regards to Angie."

"I'll do that, Frank."

Zeke hung up the phone and turned his chair so that he was looking out the large picture window into the courtyard. He spent a lot of his office time enjoying the garden and watching his family, who spent many of their afternoons there.

After the scare with Lorenzo's heart, he'd turned everything over to Zeke. He'd insisted that all he wanted to do was to stay home and be entertained by the children.

Watching him now, Zeke could well believe him. Linda and Connie sat in their tiny chairs at his feet while he read to them. Tyler sat on his lap, nodding off to sleep. Angie was nearby, mending one of the children's clothing, listening and smiling at Lorenzo's dramatic interpretation of a well-known children's classic.

Zeke waited until Angie glanced up. He waved, catching her eye, and motioned for her to come inside. After placing the mending next to her chair, she got up and headed toward the door of the salon. By the time she reached the hallway, he was waiting for her.

"What is it? Is something wrong?"

He shook his head and, taking her by the hand, led her upstairs.

"Zeke? Where are we going?"

"I thought we needed to rest. Lorenzo has the children enthralled. They'll be just fine."

"Oh, but I—"

"Oh, but you have to make sure I don't have nightmares. I sleep much better with my arms around you."

"You're so silly." She shook her head in mock despair.

As soon as they reached their room, he insisted she get comfortable. His idea of her comfort was to carefully take off every piece of her clothing, despite her attempt to slap his hands away.

"I like to look at you, okay? I love to see the baby. Relax, will you? I'm not going to molest you."

"That will be a first."

"You've got a smart mouth, woman. Anyone ever tell you that?"

She smiled, and allowed him to lead her to the bed. She stretched out on the bed and he curled around her. "I learned everything I know from you," she admitted, sighing as he began to rub her back in the exact place it ached.

"You've taught me more."

"Oh, sure I have."

"You have. It scares me to think that we might not have ended up together."

"I'm just glad you were sent down here to work for Tio. Otherwise we would never have met."

"And that would have been the greatest tragedy of all," he murmured, holding her close to him and stroking the curve of her body that sheltered another new life.

Frank's call had reminded him of his old way of life. He had heard the envy in Frank's voice. He didn't blame him. He wouldn't give up what he had now for any other life-style.

Life was good. Love was a gift he'd never thought to have. It had changed him, forced him to grow and to accept his vulnerability.

The rewards had been worth it. Tucking Angie closer against him, he fell asleep with a smile on his face.

*   *   *   *   *

Take 4 bestselling love stories FREE

Plus get a FREE surprise gift!

Relive the romance...
Harlequin and Silhouette
are proud to present

A program of collections of three complete novels by the most requested authors with the most requested themes. Be sure to look for one volume each month with three complete novels by top name authors.

In June: **NINE MONTHS** Penny Jordan
                              Stella Cameron
                              Janice Kaiser

Three women pregnant and alone. But a lot can happen in nine months!

In July: **DADDY'S**   Kristin James
           HOME   Naomi Horton
                         Mary Lynn Baxter

Daddy's Home... and his presence is long overdue!

In August: **FORGOTTEN** Barbara Kaye
           PAST   Pamela Browning
                         Nancy Martin

Do you dare to create a future if you've forgotten the past?

Available at your favorite retail outlet.

HARLEQUIN   Silhouette

Silhouette Books
is proud to present
our best authors,
their best books...
and the best in
your reading pleasure!

Throughout 1993, look for exciting
books by these top names in
contemporary romance:

DIANA PALMER—
Fire and Ice in June

ELIZABETH LOWELL—
Fever in July

CATHERINE COULTER—
Afterglow in August

LINDA HOWARD—
Come Lie With Me in September

When it comes to passion,
we wrote the book.

BOBT2

SILHOUETTE® Desire®

RED, WHITE AND BLUE...
Six sexy, hardworking, hometown hunks who were born and bred in the USA!

NEED PROTECTION?
Then you must read ZEKE #793 by Annette Broadrick
July's Man of the Month

NEED TO TAKE THE PLUNGE?
Then dive into BEN #794 by Karen Leabo

NEED TO GET AWAY?
Then sail away with DEREK #795 by Leslie Davis Guccione

NEED TO FIND YOUR ROOTS?
Then dig into CAMERON #796 by Beverly Barton

NEED A MAN?
Then warm up with JAKE #797 by Helen R. Myers

NEED A HAND?
Then you need to meet WILL #798 by Kelly Jamison

Desire invites you to meet these sexy, down-home guys! These hunks are HOT and will make you pledge allegiance to the all-American man!

SDRWB